FATAL CONSEQUENCES

A CONSEQUENCES NOVEL
BOOK 3

AMANDA SIEGRIST

McCord Family Novel

Protecting You

Trust in Love

Deserving You

Always Kind of Love

Finding You

Dare You to Love

Mona & Mason

The Paranormal Chronicles, Volume I

Perfect For You Novel

The Wrong Brother

The Right Time

The Easy Part

The Hard Choice

Psychic Love Novel

Exploding Love

Captured Love

Slaying Love Novel

Won't Let You Go

Doomed Love

Deadly Crazy

Evidence of Sin

Finding Redemption

Obsessed Hope

Short Stories

Paint By Murder

Follow Me, Sweet Darling

Sleighville Novel

Dashing Through the Fear

Here Comes Chaos

The Last Noel

Standalone Novel

The Danger with Love

Conquering Fear Novel

Co-written with Jane Blythe

Drowning in You

Out of the Darkness

Closing In

PROLOGUE

Five years ago...

A HAND SLAPPED her fingers away.

"Don't touch that."

Junelle turned to her brother, cocking a brow. "It's my birthday. I think I can eat a piece of my own birthday cake."

Jason wiggled a finger in her face. "The party hasn't started yet. Birthday or not, I'll break your little finger if you touch it. Mom worked hard on that cake."

Chuckling, always loving a good challenge with her brother, she swiped her finger with quick precision across the side of the cake. The icing melted on her tongue, the sweetness filling her up.

"Mom did an excellent job on the icing."

Rolling his eyes and shaking his head, he swiveled the cake around so no one would be able to see the indentation. "You just had to do it."

Her finger, now free of icing, waved mockingly in his face. "Gonna break it?"

"No. I'm gonna go find Rider to settle you down." He

shook his head again and walked away before she could respond.

Rider.

Her brother's best friend.

The man who made her heart go pitter-patter daily, whether or not he was even in front of her.

The man who she would always love.

The man who had no clue she held a spark of interest toward him.

Recently turned twenty-two and still pining over her brother's best friend. Pathetic. They'd been best friends since she was five, so one would think she would've gotten over her crush by now. Especially since he never saw her as a potential girlfriend.

Nothing she ever did gained his attention. The tight little dresses she wore. Of course, nothing too revealing to say she was easy. She didn't want to portray that to Rider. Or any man, for that matter.

Sweet, simple smiles thrown his way. The kind that lit up his face anytime another woman flashed him one. No reaction when she did though.

Even the lingering hugs. The ones where she couldn't bear to let go right away. He always chuckled, then pried her away like an annoying little sister.

That's all he saw her as.

Now she was turning twenty-two, about to graduate from college, and the big wide world was waiting for her. Available men were waiting for her. How long could she wait for Rider to notice her as a woman? Sure, he was twenty-seven. There was a five-year age-gap, but that wasn't monstrous. It wouldn't be frowned upon by most people. She didn't get it.

And damn it.

It was her birthday.

It was her cake.

A warm hand grabbed hers before she could take another dabble of icing. Hot, soothing breath trickled down her neck. "You're not supposed to touch the cake."

Wondering how long he'd hold her hand, she was afraid to look at him. The very man she'd been daydreaming about, as if she conjured him herself, was so close she wanted to cry from the sensation of his soft touch. "Says who?"

"Says me. You don't want to hurt your mom's feelings after she worked so hard, do you?"

Lifting her gaze, she gave a half-hearted grin. "Of course not."

"What's the matter, June Bug? You look sad."

I love you and you don't see me as anything but a little sister. "I'm not sad. Don't listen to Jason or whatever he might've said."

Why would her brother think Rider could calm her down? Well, he could. Perhaps it was just obvious. Jason always ran to Rider when he couldn't calm her down himself. One simple touch and a smile from Rider, and all her worries always washed away. It was so easy to get lost in his striking blue eyes.

Did that mean her brother knew how she felt? Did Rider?

Obviously not, otherwise he would've made a move by now. Or told her to stop her silly wishing they could be together.

Swiping a lock of hair behind her ear, Rider then tugged on her hand. "Come on. I have something to cheer you up."

"I'm not sad!"

He raised a brow as if he knew that was a lie. "Follow

me, June Bug. A special girl like you deserves an early birthday present. You want it or not?"

A special girl? What did that even mean? He still refused to see her as a woman. Perhaps she needed to start stripping in front of him and offer her body. He wouldn't mistake what that meant.

"I want it." *I want you.*

Smiling, he pulled her away from the living room where her party was all set up. The guests wouldn't arrive for another half hour. For the next thirty minutes, all she wanted was to spend it with Rider.

To her surprise, he walked into her bedroom, at the very end of the hallway, and shut the door. He'd never done that before.

Without warning, he dropped his hand and shifted away from her. "June Bug..."

Her heart melted at his soft tone and by the nickname he'd given her when she was sixteen. No one else called her June Bug. Only Rider. As if she were *his* June Bug.

The worry that popped up between his brows made her heart skip a beat. He said he wanted to give her a present. This didn't look like that's what he was about to do.

"Now I feel like I should ask you what's the matter. Are you okay, Rider?"

Like a light switch, his face bloomed with delight. "I'm perfect." He hesitated. "You're perfect." Slipping a hand in his pocket, he withdrew a tiny box. "For you."

Tiny tremors tickled her fingers as she reached for the box. Their fingers grazed. It's as if fireworks exploded. Or maybe that was her nerves trying to break free.

His smile never wavered as she opened the box.

A slow breath left her body as she stared at the beautiful

necklace. A sparkling silver chain with two delicate hearts attached together. She had never seen anything so precious in her life. Well, in her hand anyway, and given to her by a guy.

What did it mean?

Rider had never given her anything like this before.

His warm hand enclosed around her hand holding the box. "Do you like it?"

She met his gaze again and nodded. "I love it. But why would you give me something so...beautiful?"

He cupped her cheeks, his baby-blue eyes blazing with what she could only decipher as desire. It couldn't be. She must be dreaming. Maybe she fainted and this would all disappear when she regained her senses. If that were the case, she never wanted to wake up.

"Because you're beautiful. And I can't seem to hold myself back any longer."

"What?"

This wasn't happening. She had to be dreaming. She knocked her head or something. Rider only treated her this way in her dreams. Did she die? Maybe she was allergic to something that had been in the icing and she'd gone into anaphylactic shock. Yes. That's what happened.

"June Bug, I want you. Your brother would kill me if he knew."

She couldn't believe her ears. This was real. Rider was admitting to having feelings for her.

Yes!

"Then what are you waiting for? Kiss me, Rider. Because I've wanted you since I was like ten." Because the first five years he'd been in her life, she'd been too young to even want him around. Then one day, it was as if the shutters over her eyes had been unveiled.

Chuckling, he pulled her closer. "I know. You have made it very hard to resist you."

His kiss silenced any other words.

From there, their relationship bloomed. Secretly, anyway. For a whole month they kept the love developing between them to themselves. Despite that, they were inseparable. Most of the time. Her brother had been around a few times and neither of them were quite comfortable sharing the news they were together.

Together!

She still couldn't get over it. Her birthday, when he kissed her for the first time, was a memory she knew she'd never forget. Ever.

His touch. So sweet. So soft.

Last week, he made love to her for the first time. It had been the most erotic, beautiful thing she'd ever experienced. She knew she hadn't been his first, but he'd been hers. And she cherished that knowledge every day. Rider was hers!

His hands. His touch. His words. They all painted a picture that said he cared. Perhaps even that he loved her. Though they hadn't exchanged those elusive words yet.

She hoped he loved her because she had loved him for so long she couldn't even remember the exact moment she fell in love.

"Thanks, Barney. You're the best." Junelle smiled at the best barista ever. She always came to the same java shop to get her coffee. And she always tried to come when she knew Barney would be working.

He winked. "Only the best for the sweetest woman I know."

Chuckling, she waved and headed out the door.

She had about an hour before her afternoon class. She wasn't too hungry, but perhaps she'd stop by Finnegan's and grab one of their sandwiches. They made the best sandwiches in the world.

Yeah, she'd do that and then head to class.

Her steps slowed as she neared the corner.

No.

It couldn't be.

He wouldn't.

Yet, he was.

Heartache filled her soul as she walked closer. Then betrayal and disgust filtered in. Followed by an intense fury she'd never felt before. How dare he!

"Rider, what a surprise?" Junelle said in the most delicate tone she could manage, which was pretty darn sweet to her. They wouldn't think she was dying inside.

Rider turned around and dropped his hand that had been around the redhead's waist. "June Bug!"

"Aww! You're so cute when you act surprised." Junelle forced a charming smile out, except there was nothing pleasant beneath it. She knew he could see the turmoil and rage swimming in her veins.

With a quick twist of her wrist, she took the cover off her coffee cup and tossed the contents at him.

"June Bug, wait!" Rider jumped from the coffee hitting him square in the chest like a bullseye had been attached, then rushed after her.

Wait?

Who did he think he was? She wasn't waiting on him for anything. Not ever again.

That redhead had been gorgeous, the way her hair swept around her shoulders, the dress skintight to her body showing all her delicious curves.

No. She wouldn't think about it. Any of it.

"June Bug—"

She tore his hand off her arm. "Don't talk to me. Don't call me. Don't ever come near me again. I'd hate to have to tell Jason."

His face became hard as granite. "I don't even get a chance to explain. That's not right."

"Neither was your arm around another woman. I've been such a fool. I won't make the same mistake twice."

Looking guilty, he glanced behind him and then back at her. "I need to explain. I can't right now, but later. Later we'll talk." He stepped forward and grabbed her arm. With a gentle grip, but still firmly. She'd have to tug to get free. "We will talk. But nothing you saw is what it seems."

1

"I'M SORRY, WHAT, CAPTAIN?"

Rider had to have misheard what he thought he heard. He hadn't been involved in narcotics since he'd been a rookie. And he'd done it the one time.

And that one time had ruined his life irrevocably. He'd lost the woman he loved by one tiny lie. Not something he wanted to think about right now. Or ever.

"They need help with an undercover case. They're strapped right now. I know you've done undercover before. It's been a few years, but you did a damn good job on that case."

A damn good job? Yeah, of messing up his life.

The torture. The pain etched on her face at what she thought he did. He would never touch another woman. Never! Since that day, he'd never been able to get her devastated face out of his mind. And damn it, he had tried. So many times.

He loved her so much it hurt to breathe sometimes. He'd never stopped loving her, even after all this time. She'd shoved him out of her life without giving him a chance to explain. Of course, it wasn't as if he could explain the real reason he'd let that woman cling to him. He couldn't have told her he was undercover trying to take down one of the largest drug dealers in the city. He couldn't have told her that the woman he had his arm around was nothing more than a means to an end to make the bust.

He hadn't been able to tell her shit.

All he ever wanted was to be a detective. To solve crimes. To help people. To make a difference.

Being a beat cop had sucked at times. But that's where everyone started. Nobody magically moved into detective status with a snap of their fingers. He had been prepared to crawl his way up the ladder. Because being a detective was his dream.

Just like his dad.

Three years on the force and given the opportunity to go undercover to show off his skills, he couldn't pass it up. He couldn't say no.

Well, he could now. Because he worked homicide. He was a detective.

"I'll pass."

"I need you on this, Rider."

"I can't."

Captain Wilson stared at him for the longest time. "I've heard a few rumors."

Okay. He could imagine what those rumors were. He wasn't going to ask though.

"That you've been withdrawn. Not yourself. I have to agree."

He wouldn't disagree either. Getting stabbed so damn close to his heart and nearly dying changed a person. It made them reevaluate their life. He had decided, after much contemplation lying in the hospital, his life was shit. And he should've died that day. That was the conclusion he'd come up with. What was the point of anything anymore?

But even if that hadn't happened, he wouldn't have taken the undercover gig. Not after what happened the last time.

"Which means I'm not up to the task, Captain. So the answer is no."

Captain Wilson leaned back in his chair, sighing. "I see I'm not going to win this argument. I have to agree with your assessment. You're not up to the task. I'm not even sure you're up to the task of anything at this point."

He sat up straighter in his chair. "Now, wait a minute, Cap—"

"You nearly died and I'm not sure you've processed that. Perhaps you need to take a step back. I let you come back too soon."

From his job? From his livelihood? From the one thing keeping him sane? From the only thing forcing him to wake up every day?

Hell no!

"I'm fine. I work my cases with precision and all the due diligence they deserve. I'm focused. But I don't want to go undercover. That's a whole other ball game I don't want to play around with."

Captain Wilson didn't answer his plea. Instead, he grabbed the phone and asked Detective Stromberg and Powell to join them. What the hell was his captain up to?

The two men entered without a sound and stood by the door. He didn't even look in their direction or offer a greeting.

"Stromberg!" his captain barked. "What are your thoughts on Rider and his performance lately?"

Was he serious?

Rider turned his gaze toward Stromberg, cocking a brow.

Challenging him to say the wrong thing. He was done caring what others thought of him, but he would fight anyone that tried to take his livelihood away. Stromberg would be wise to choose his words carefully.

Damn the captain!

Putting his fellow detectives under the spotlight. He'd been a jackass to everyone the last four months since he'd been stabbed. The other day, Stromberg tried to offer him an olive branch and invited him to watch a baseball game. He loved baseball. But he'd declined—and was rather curt about it.

No matter how hard he glared at them, he knew they were about to throw him under the bus. He could sense it like a live wire was about to scorch his skin.

"He's laser focused and doing his job, sir."

Captain Wilson growled, as if unsatisfied with that answer. Rider wanted to clap Stromberg on the back for being on his side. He understood the silent message.

"Powell?"

Detective Powell, or rather Tate, as most people called him, cleared his throat. "He's been an asshole, but he gets shit done."

Tate produced a shit-eating grin as if he enjoyed getting him in trouble. Stromberg was side-eyeing Tate, like he couldn't believe he said that.

"Okay, Rider. You're getting glowing recommendations from your co-workers."

He damn near chuckled. Tate called him an asshole. How was that glowing?

"But what I'm actually hearing is you're so focused on your cases, you're not taking care of yourself."

"What is this, Captain? Are you suspending me for doing my job?" He stood up so fast, his chair scraped backward against the floor, nearly toppling over. "If you're taking my badge from me for not going undercover, then do it!"

"I'm not taking your badge from you. But you will be working with Stromberg and Powell from here on out. When Powell tells me you're not an asshole anymore, you can go back to being solo."

He glared at the two men he thought were his friends, then back at his captain. "You're giving me babysitters because one of them thinks I'm an asshole?"

"Yes. And you are being an asshole. I don't like it. You never were one until..."

Yeah, until he knocked on heaven's door and wished like hell he would've gotten an answer.

"Get out and go do your job. With those two!"

Captain Wilson went back to the paperwork splattered across his desk, effectively dismissing them. He pushed by Tate, not even caring he'd smacked Tate's shoulder hard with his own. Though he should've because a shot of pain hit his chest. Right where the knife had gone in with the second sweep. One would think his shoulder would hurt more where he'd been stabbed first, but no, the wound in his chest gave him more fits than anything.

He swore he could feel the knife still embedded in his chest at times, like a phantom pain. Not that he'd lost a limb or needed a new heart. But the pain was always there, even more when he exerted more energy than he should.

Stromberg and Tate gathered by his desk, forcing him to look up at them.

"Piss off."

Then he put his attention back to his latest case.

"Hey, man, we don't like this any more than you, but—"

"But what, Stromberg?" Rider asked, glaring. "You didn't give a damn a few months ago when the captain suspended you. You kept on working. And guess what? I kept my damn mouth shut. You can give me the same courtesy and let me do my own thing."

"Except we're not going to do that," Tate replied. That annoying shit-eating grin was back. "While I hate it as much as you, I'm not going to ignore what the captain said. I'm sorry I didn't lie like Stromberg. We wouldn't be in this situation if I had."

"Hey," Stromberg pouted. "I didn't lie."

"You omitted the truth. Same thing." Tate jerked a finger at him. "He has been an asshole and you know it. Even he knows it."

Rider slumped into his chair, unable to argue because Tate was right. He couldn't even say he tried not to be an asshole. He just didn't care about anything anymore.

"We're working together until *I* tell the captain you're not an asshole. We're not arguing about it anymore." Tate's harsh expression and clipped words said Rider shouldn't even waste his breath disagreeing. While he wanted to, the zeal to do it wasn't there.

"Yo, Tate. Got a dead body for you. Her name's Molly. Here's the address," Roco said, handing him a piece of paper. Rider didn't miss the way he snickered as he walked away. Though Tate must've because he didn't call him out on it. Tate was never one to let anything like that slide.

"Let's go," Tate ordered, waving the piece of paper. "Work calls."

SHE LET the warmth of her brother's arm envelope her, yet didn't drop her head to his shoulder like she wanted to. If she did, she'd turn into a blubbering mess.

"I called the cops."

That had her jerking out of his arms. "Why'd you do that?"

Jason swung a hand to her beloved dog, now lying mangled in the yard. Dead. "Umm...it's not normal for a dog to be murdered, Junelle. That's why."

Well, she couldn't argue with that logic. It's just...she didn't like the cops. Not for any nefarious reason or anything.

She didn't want to see *his* face ever again. If the cops were called, there was always that small chance he'd be the one to show up.

It didn't take long for an officer to arrive. Jason did most of the talking as she was too choked up to say much. She had no idea what the officer did after that, but he told them he'd be back and went to the front of her house. She could do nothing but stare at her beloved baby. Not even Jason could tear her away, and she knew he wanted to.

A throat cleared. She looked over at the officer, wondering how much time had passed since he had walked away. "The detectives are here. I'll bring them back here."

Detectives?

That seemed extreme. A little overkill, but what did she know about police procedure? Nothing, that's what. But she wouldn't argue about it. They were the professionals, not her. Though her brother looked a bit surprised himself.

She felt tears brimming and turned around. First, she had to compose herself, then she'd face whoever came into the yard.

"It's going to be okay, Junelle. I promise." But Jason's promise fell short. Because if things were okay, her sweet fur baby would've never been harmed.

She was an adult, and she'd act like it. There would be

no crying until she was alone and could do it without anyone seeing or hearing her fall to pieces. Even her brother.

She swiveled back around, finding a smile out of nowhere.

Jason rolled his eyes. "No one expects you to be happy. Stop trying to pretend you are."

The smile disappeared. He was right, of course. And thank goodness he'd come home with her after they had lunch. She had wanted to give him his birthday present he forgot the other day and instead, they had come home to heartbreak.

"Mr. and Mrs. Swanson, these are the detectives that will be handling your case," the officer said, leading the gentlemen behind him.

Seriously! Talk about being glad he wouldn't be handling it.

Because what an idiot!

Jason was her brother! Mr. and Mrs. Swanson...so ridiculous to even think about. If she wasn't so distraught, she would've busted out laughing at the notion.

He stepped to the side and her heart lodged in her throat.

Of all the times...

Of all the people who could've responded...

Rider.

He looked just as shocked.

"Holy shit, man," Jason exclaimed. "I can't believe it's you."

Rider offered a short grin, but it was so fleeting she wasn't sure if it had been real. "Hey, Jason. I'm sorry it's under these circumstances."

"Yeah, dude, me too. I've been trying to call you the last

few months. I can't believe—" Jason stopped speaking and looked at her. "I'm sorry, Junelle. I'll chat with him later."

"I'm Detective Tate Powell, my partner Detective Stromberg, and you already seem to know Detective Rider." Tate glanced at her sweet fur baby on the ground. "Where is the other body?"

"What do you mean?" Jason asked.

The officer cleared his throat. "The dog is the body. Her name is Molly."

Junelle wanted to take a step back when the rage lit up Detective Powell's face. But she didn't because she knew that anger wasn't directed at her. The officer was in deep shit and she couldn't find an ounce of remorse for him. She had a feeling he deserved it.

"Can you explain to me, Officer Dorenson, why three detectives had to come for a dead dog?" Tate asked through gritted teeth.

"No, sir, I can't. I thought you and Stromberg would show up. Not Rider."

Detective Stromberg laughed, then coughed to cover it up. Then laughed again. "I keep telling you, Tate, to make nice with everyone. This is what happens when you don't. They mess with you."

She could discern from the short conversation that detectives didn't handle deceased pets. And why would they? It did seem preposterous for them to be here. Obviously, some of the officers were having fun at their expense. Of course, she didn't find it funny. At all. It was her beautiful baby at the center of it all.

But whatever. She'd let it go. She wouldn't make a stink about it. Because she was using all her energy not to fall into a blubbering mess. Maybe she'd make a stink about it later when she had full control of her emotions.

But the bigger question that boggled her mind was why Rider showed up with them if they hadn't expected him to? Did he recognize her address and responded because of that? Did that mean he'd kept tabs on her and knew where she had moved?

Why wouldn't he look at her? In the eyes?

Five long years and she still hadn't gotten over him. After what he had done to her, she should've been able to with ease. While she liked to pretend she had moved on, she knew he would always hold a piece of her heart.

But it was better he didn't look directly at her. Because he would see the hatred she had for him. And she'd see his guilt. Not something she needed to add to her emotional plate.

"And I'm the one considered an asshole," Rider muttered under his breath.

Odd thing to say.

"You *are* an asshole, so you're taking the lead on this case." Tate swept an arm to the dog and took a step back.

Rider didn't grin or laugh or show any expression that he thought anything was funny.

Not even Detective Stromberg, who had laughed before, let loose the joyous sound. He looked frightened, in fact. As if a brawl would start any moment between his two colleagues.

Rider took a step closer, nodding. "I have no problem with that. Jason was my best friend."

"Is. I *am* your best friend," her brother interjected, growling low with frustration.

Rider made no comment to correct him, demanding that he wasn't. He wouldn't even look Jason in the eye. Coward!

"You're not needed any longer, Officer. Get the hell out of here," Detective Powell snapped.

"You almost sounded like a New Yorker there," Detective Stromberg said.

That comment produced another tiny smile from Rider, fleeting once again. "That man will never be a true New Yorker. Never."

"For that, I'll prove you wrong."

Rider rolled his eyes and directed his attention back to Jason. "What happened?"

Jason pointed to her. "Molly's Junelle's dog. We came home from lunch and found her like this."

The man who had captured her heart only to break it with no remorse finally looked at her. No guilt detected. And she couldn't find the energy to display her rage.

"I'm sorry for your loss."

His baby-blue eyes penetrated straight to her soul. Making her wish deep down in the pit of her stomach things had turned out differently between them. Although his words sounded sincere, she didn't want his sympathy. She didn't want anything from him.

"I'd prefer it if you didn't work this case."

"Junelle!" Jason admonished.

Rider flinched, closing his eyes. When he reopened them, he'd gone back to not looking at her.

"You're stuck with me like I'm stuck with these two until I'm told otherwise." Rider flicked an aimless gesture at his colleagues. "So I'm going to ask you questions whether you like it or not."

Her gaze glided to Molly and the tears threatened to flow once again.

"Why don't we go inside and do that?" Jason motioned toward the sliding glass door. Then guided her inside when everyone agreed.

They took a seat at the small table she had in the

kitchen. Rider sat across from her, which she was grateful for. Jason was to her left with Detective Stromberg to her right and the other one next to his other side.

"Do you know anyone who would want to hurt you or your dog?"

She shrugged.

"Any complainants against Molly?"

"No."

"Did she excessively bark or get out of the house frequently?"

"No."

Molly had been the sweetest, most lovable dog on the planet. Her backyard was tiny. Not surprising as she lived in the city. Of course it was fenced in. But she could've let Molly roam free and she wouldn't have strayed from her property. She had trained her well. Something she had been so proud of when Molly had graduated obedience training school. They'd even given out certificates that she had hung on the wall. Proudly displayed in her living room.

"Did you leave her in the backyard when you left?"

"No."

"Junelle," Jason huffed. "Try elaborating a little bit more than that. He's trying to help."

They were literally yes or no questions. She didn't have to elaborate if she didn't want to.

"Molly...Molly looked..."

She glanced up at Rider when he stalled in finishing his statement. Odd. He looked on the verge of tears himself. He was rubbing his chest with vigorous motions back and forth. When he saw her noticing what he was doing, he stopped.

"She looks like she's been stabbed repeatedly." His weird moment of vulnerability was over. "We all realize this is a dog, but if that was a human, I'd call that a crime of passion.

Someone was very angry when they killed Molly. Who could you have made that angry?"

Her brother was going to kill her. Maybe even Rider...if he still cared about her. Doubtful.

She stood up from the table and walked out of the room. She heard muffled whispers but didn't try to listen to what they were saying. The papers she'd shoved in her desk drawer scorched her skin the moment she picked them up. She wanted to hide them back where she found them. Instead, she walked back into the kitchen and laid them on the table.

"I don't know who the person is, but I assume it's the same person who wrote these letters that hurt Molly."

2
_____

RIDER'S hands trembled as he picked up a letter, and he hated the sign of weakness. Then he damn near crumbled it after he read the degrading, vile words.

"Stop!" he yelled when Tate went to reach for one. "They should be handled as evidence. It appears June—" He nearly called her June Bug. "Elle has a stalker. A quite deadly one."

"Seriously, Junelle," Jason groaned. "Why wouldn't you tell me about this? How long has this been going on?"

She'd reverted to not looking at him, which was fine in his opinion. He had a hard time looking at her as well. Because all he wanted to do was pull her into his arms and never let go.

And why? She'd been the one to break things off. She had decided he didn't deserve a chance to explain anything. He shouldn't want anything to do with her, and yet, his heart beat like a stampede of rhinos. Nerves were rising to the surface as if there would be a chance to reconnect.

"Because I knew you'd overreact."

Jason threw an arm toward the sliding door. "And I

would've been right to overreact. Look what happened to Molly. That could've been you out there."

Not something Rider wanted to picture, yet that's what he did. The brutal image of her bloodied body entered his mind and refused to leave. His hands trembled again, so much that he slid them underneath the table to hide the act.

"Are you dating anyone?" Stromberg asked, and Rider could've hugged him for asking the question instead of him. Because he was dying to know as well, and he didn't think she'd like answering him.

"No."

"Anyone recently where the breakup didn't go well?" Stromberg continued.

"No."

Jason huffed again. "I can't take her one-word answers. So I'll skip all the other ones you have to get straight to the point. She doesn't date. Like ever. As her older brother who grills all the men she brings home, I should be happy. Instead, I'm annoyed and worried and wondering what the hell is wrong with my sister that she doesn't want to date anyone. That I don't get to grill anyone."

"Jason," she hissed, her cheeks blooming a bright red.

"Well, it's true."

Rider knew the reason she didn't date. At least, the conceited part of himself assumed why she didn't. Because of him. Because of the way he broke her heart. Or so she thought with the inaccurate details she had before her.

It hadn't been his fault!

He'd been undercover. He'd been doing his job. Never in a million years, for any reason, would he have touched another woman.

Yet, she never gave him a chance to explain. Not that he would've been able to give her the real answer right away.

He would've had to lie until the case had completed. It had taken him another two months to close it. Two months of lying...that he never had to do because she closed the door on their relationship. Without even flinching. Which told him she had never cared for him as much as he had for her.

"That's still a damning answer in itself," Stromberg noted. "Who has asked you out and you rejected them?"

"I mean, lately, no one. There have been guys over the years that have asked me out."

Rider removed the notepad he carried around everywhere and his pen from the pocket inside his jacket, pushing it across the table. "We need all their names."

She stared at him for the longest time before she grabbed the pad and started writing.

"I'll call for forensics." Tate stood up from the table and walked outside.

"For my dog?"

"Yes, for your dog," Rider answered with clipped words. Was she serious? Could she be that dense? "If you weren't worried about these letters before, you should be now. You should've told your brother! This could escalate to you being the one butchered outside. Stop acting like an idiot."

At his harshness, she jumped up from the table and left the room, her shoulders visibly shaking. He'd reduced her to the tears she had fought so hard outside to hold in.

He hated himself even more than he did this morning. And that was saying something because he truly despised himself.

"Geez, Rider. Go easy on her," Jason said. "What the hell happened to you? Five years ago, you upped and walked out of my life. You ignored my calls. You pretended I didn't exist. Now here you are and you're speaking to Junelle like she never mattered to you. If this threatening shit wasn't going on, I would think you didn't care about her. But I know you do because you're worried and it's coming out all wrong. That's the only reason I'm not knocking you flat on your ass right now."

Then Jason left the room too.

"Don't," he commanded, lifting a hand in the air for Stromberg to keep his mouth shut.

But when in the hell did Stromberg, or Tate for that matter, ever do what anyone wanted them to do?

"I think you care for her. I saw the way you looked when her brother said she doesn't date. Does he know you love her?"

Rider shoved his face into his hands, groaning. "Stop it, Stromberg."

"Hey, I won't meddle. But I want you to know I get it. That gut-wrenching feeling that you can't have the one you love. I get it."

He dropped his hands. "You have Briella. You couldn't possibly understand."

"Yeah, but I didn't have her in the beginning."

"I said I didn't want to have this conversation."

Stromberg put up his hands in a surrender gesture.

Tate took that opportunity to walk back inside. "What did I miss?"

"Not much."

At least Stromberg had the courtesy not to spill his secret to Tate. But no doubt he'd do it later when Rider wasn't around. Those two didn't keep secrets from each other. He used to be like that with Jason.

Forensics came with questioning looks when they saw the dog. But Rider demanded an autopsy and to treat Molly like a human. He wanted the entire house swept for a scrap of evidence and how the suspect gained entry. A quick walk around the house showed no signs of forced entry. He wanted answers so he could find the bastard who wanted to hurt his June Bug.

No. Not his June Bug.

Not anymore.

They also took the letters.

They decided they'd canvas the neighborhood and find someone who might've seen something. People were nosy these days. Someone had to have seen something. Tate and Stromberg left first, forcing him to say the goodbyes. Jason had returned to the kitchen, but Junelle still hadn't reappeared.

"We'll be back. As soon as I know anything from forensics, I'll call you. Make sure she gives us that list of guys who asked her out."

"I wish it were for a different reason. I tried calling months ago. I wanted you there for my parents' fortieth wedding anniversary. I've wanted you around for a lot of things."

And he was sorry he couldn't be. But the moment Junelle broke it off, he knew he wouldn't be able to be around Jason. Not for a moment. He would've caved telling him what happened and then he would've lost him anyway. Jason would never stand for him dating his sister.

Lost the woman he loved and lost his best friend.

"What happened to you? What happened to my best friend?"

"I'm sorry I hurt you. That I continue to hurt you. I'm sorry. I'll call you about the case."

Then he turned and left before Jason could interrogate him any further.

They interviewed the neighbors up and down the street, but nobody had seen anything suspicious. There were no cameras focused on Junelle's house to show the culprit in the act, though a few neighbors had security cameras and said they would check them out for anything suspicious. Rider wouldn't hold his breath on that, but he thanked them nonetheless.

They headed back to the precinct where they first gave Roco a severe berating. All the asshole could do was laugh. They all thought it was funny sending them on a murder case—a murdered dog case.

Toward the end, even Tate and Stromberg chuckled.

He didn't utter one sound.

Because if they hadn't played the trick on them, he wouldn't have gotten handed the case, and he would've never known Junelle was in danger. While she might not want anything to do with him, he'd protect her with his life.

Hell, he'd protected Briella with his life—damn near losing it—and he didn't love her. So yeah, he'd protect Junelle, even if she didn't want his protection. Not that he'd be much of a protector. He failed with Briella.

They went to the lab where all the letters were bagged and tagged, reading each one. The more he read, the more the anger swelled inside. When he got his hands on this bastard...well, he was contemplating murder for the first time in his life.

The vulgar things he wrote. The descriptions of how he'd rape her. Though the bastard hadn't used that vile word. His sexual descriptions painted the picture though. The weird mentions of where she'd been as if he followed her around twenty-four-seven. That had him telling patrol to up their rounds in her neighborhood. He wanted her protected at all times. Of course, he knew Jason wouldn't leave her side. Not until this asshole was caught. Good thing about that. Because if Jason hadn't, he would've stepped up for the job. No doubt with her kicking and screaming.

By eight o'clock, he was ready to go home and crash. He kept his ass planted in his seat, searching the list of names she'd given them. Jason had called him, not her. Part of him had been relieved he didn't have to speak to her. But the other part of him had been disappointed. It told him where he stood with her. Off-limits and far, far away.

"Take a break, Rider."

He didn't look up at Stromberg or even acknowledge him.

"You can't help her if you're dead on your feet."

"I need to find this asshole."

"And we will. But you can't if you're falling apart. Let's go home."

He slumped in his chair, casting a glance Stromberg's way. "You know I'll keep working at home."

"Fine by me. At least you went home." Then he grinned and waited for Rider to pack up, not letting the issue lie.

And Rider did exactly what he said he'd do.

He went back to work. Back to the grind. At home.

HE WATCHED from his usual spot, spying on Junelle. Despite the terrible altercation with her dog, she didn't appear to be too frightened. She hadn't even closed the curtains in the living room or her bedroom. He'd watched her cry in her bedroom. When she'd been standing. As soon as she flung herself to her bed, he'd lost visual of her.

Damn it. He wanted to watch her cry. He wanted to see the torment she was in. Because then she'd know how he felt. The devastating despair in his heart and soul.

When he broke into her house this morning—so painfully easy too—he never intended to harm her sweet dog. The fluffy mongrel had approached him unafraid, looking for a rub. He'd obliged, of course. He loved dogs. Though he was more of a cat person.

The house felt empty without her presence, but every room he'd ventured to spoke such volumes. Every imprint of her was in each corner.

It disgusted him to have it thrown in his face like that!

That damn dog had followed him like he owned the damn thing.

When he walked out to the backyard, the dog darted outside with him. The action had made the anger spring free.

Why did her dog seem to love him and she didn't? Junelle wouldn't even give him the time of day, while her dog wanted all the affection he could give.

Once his anger had been released, there had been no way to contain it. The knife he'd brought appeared in his hand.

Then the dog was dead.

And he'd had blood all over him. He hadn't prepared for that. And he prided himself on being prepared. Always. His nerves had run rampant the entire way to his car that someone would see him. Would know the horror he committed.

When he got home, his own beloved pet, Charles, his sweet tabby cat, brushed up against his leg. He knew not in comfort that Charles sensed he needed it. But because he always greeted him when he came home.

The clothes went into the trash and the shower he took was so long, the hot water left his skin red. Then he cried at the loss of innocence he'd taken.

He hadn't meant to kill the dog.

But now that it was dead, she'd know the pain he suffered every single day. The trip hadn't been useless after all.

Then he dressed, fed Charles, and went back to his spot to spy on her.

The anguish and sadness as she cried brought his delight to the surface. Yes. That's what he wanted to see. That's what he wanted to feel. She brought this on herself.

How could he keep her pain going?

Simple death for her would not suffice.

She needed to agonize in the torrent of pain. So she'd know how he felt when she treated him with such disregard.

RIDER GLANCED at the door when he heard a loud knock. Then he turned his attention back to his computer.

Whoever it was could piss off. He had too much work to do. And if it was Stromberg or Tate, he'd see their ugly mugs enough tomorrow.

Another knock sounded. Even louder this time.

"Stop being an asshole!"

That had him jerking his attention to the door again.

Jason.

Well, he couldn't ignore him. Not after what happened at Junelle's. If he didn't have to continue to interact with them, he would've kept on working and pretended he had never heard a sound. But since he had to, he opened the door.

Jason brushed past him without a hello. Rider made his way to his computer, closing the top. Something he should've done before he answered the door. Jason didn't need to see what he was working on. It would intensify his anger.

"Want a beer?"

He could be cordial when he wanted to be. Even though he'd walked away from Jason, they'd been best friends since they were ten. They had been through a lot together. His mom passing away from cancer. His grandpa dying shortly thereafter. Jason losing his baseball scholarship after hurting his arm at the end of their senior year. There went his dreams of becoming a pro. He never could throw the same after he had healed.

So yeah. They'd been through too much together for him not to be a little nice.

"No, I won't be here long." Jason didn't hold that same belief.

Rider inclined his head, agreeing to his terms, then leaned against his table. He had a small apartment. One bedroom and one bathroom with the kitchen, living room, and dining room all in one. It suited him. He didn't need much.

But as Jason looked around, he felt like he fell par to whatever Jason was thinking.

"I haven't heard back from forensics yet."

"That's not why I'm here."

Okay, well, he'd wait for whatever Jason was here for then. He hadn't finished going through the list of men who'd asked out Junelle Jason had sent him earlier. He imagined Jason wasn't here for that reason either.

"Why'd you disappear five years ago? You didn't even give me a reason for your abrupt silence. You just stopped talking to me. What did I do wrong?"

Damn it. Why did he have to bring this up? Why couldn't they ignore what happened and move on?

Not as friends, of course.

But for the sake of the case.

"I'm not leaving until you tell me why." Then Jason crossed his arms and got that look in his eyes Rider knew well. The only way he'd be getting Jason out of here was if he told him the truth—or physically threw him out.

"You didn't do anything wrong. It was me. I needed to walk away."

Jason shook his head, his brows furrowing low. "Not good enough. Tell me why? Whatever happened, I would've been there for you."

No, he wouldn't have. Rider slept with his sister and then, according to her, cheated on her. Jason would've beat the hell out of him.

"I have my reasons. And you can stand there all night and I'm not going to tell you why."

Throwing him out seemed to be the better option. Jason could be stubborn as hell when he wanted to be.

The muscles in Jason's cheeks bunched as the fury erupted in his gaze. "Does it have to do with Junelle?"

Rider flinched and he knew he gave it away. That he'd inadvertently said yes.

"Because she changed around the same time. Odd, uh? More closed off. Sad. Wouldn't even stay in the room when I spoke your name."

He was about to get the beating of his life, and maybe he should've gotten it over with five years ago. Except, back then, he would've fought back. He would've tried to explain the misunderstanding.

But now?

Now he'd let Jason crush him because he didn't have any energy left.

His hand reached up, rubbing against his chest, right

where the knife had pierced him. He felt the phantom pain again, as if the knife was stuck.

"You touched my sister."

He couldn't deny it. So he said nothing.

"You broke her heart."

Still couldn't deny that either. Of course, she had broken his in return.

"Funny thing is, you look just as heartbroken. How can you both be heartbroken? What the hell went wrong?"

What was Jason looking for from him? Beat his ass and get it over with.

"Rider? You better start saying something before I..."

Before he what? Kicked his ass? Yeah, that's what he was waiting for.

"I'm not going to fight you. So do what you gotta do and then leave."

Jason deflated right before him.

Then a thought ripped through his mind. "Where's Junelle? You didn't leave her alone, did you?" That straightened his stance. If Jason left her alone...

He tried to calculate how long it would take him to get to her place when laughter filled the room.

Jason's loud chuckling grated on his nerves. "I would never leave my sister in danger. Her friends came over. There's four women, one of which knows karate and a whole other host of dangerous shit." The laughter died as Jason threw a hand in his direction. "That reaction alone tells me you still care for her. So why the hell did you walk away?"

"Look, if you're going to kick my ass, do it. I have too much shit to do to keep talking about this."

"You want me to kick your ass."

His gaze glided to the floor. "It's been a long time coming. Get it over with."

Rider flinched when a hand touched his shoulder. Talk about light on his feet. He hadn't heard one sound come his way.

Of course, he shouldn't be surprised. Bryan, the man who stabbed him, had walked up behind him without him hearing a sound then too. Got the jump on him and nearly took his life.

He raised his gaze to meet Jason's. If he was going down, he'd do it like a man.

"If there is one person in this entire world that I would trust with my sister's life, it would be you. So if you think I would've hated the idea of you two dating, you're wrong. There's no better guy out there for her."

What?

No, he couldn't mean that.

"Do you think I'm stupid? Do you think I never noticed how you rarely dated much? Do you think I never saw the way you looked at her? I knew she had a puppy crush on you. She wasn't hard to read. But it took me a while to see it from you. But then I did and I wondered when the hell you were going to do something about it. Then you were gone from our lives. No warning." Jason squeezed his shoulder, right near the spot he'd taken the first stab. He winced, despite that area not giving him fits like his chest did. "So when I say I'm not leaving until you tell me why you walked away, I mean it."

There was no use avoiding this conversation. Jason would pry it out of his mouth. So he gave in.

"The night of her twenty-second birthday I gave her a present and confessed I liked her. We started dating and I felt guilty as hell keeping it from you, but I thought I had to.

I thought you'd hate the idea. At the same time, I also started working undercover to take down a gang. I wanted to make detective so bad, and I couldn't pass up the opportunity. Of course, I couldn't tell her. I couldn't tell anyone. A month later, she saw me with a woman hanging off my arm. She was a pawn to take down the gang. Nothing more. But that's not what Junelle saw. She wouldn't give me a chance to explain, not that it would've mattered. I couldn't tell her the truth. Since I knew I'd lost her, I couldn't bear to be around you. So I left. I kept my distance. There's your answer. You can go now."

"A damn misunderstanding," Jason muttered, right before he shoved his arms around him in the tightest hug he'd ever gotten from him.

Rider didn't want the embrace. He wanted to push him away, yet he found his arms going around his best friend he'd missed like hell.

They stood there for ages. For two men to hug that long, it felt awkward. Yet, he couldn't find the energy to pull away either. He had needed this. The forgiveness for hurting his sister's heart. The closeness they'd had as kids growing up. Not that they ever hugged before. But knowing Jason didn't hate him was enough to fill a tiny portion of his heart that died so long ago.

When they broke apart, Jason grinned. "Okay, I'll take one beer."

He took that opportunity to get himself together. Tears were forcing their way to the surface, and he'd be damned if he cried in front of Jason. He thought he did pretty well gaining his composure. Though when he saw Jason lounging on the couch, the same watery eyes stared at him. At least they were acting the same. Neither had to be embarrassed by their loss of control on their emotions.

He handed Jason the beer and took a seat next to him. He'd always had his couch turned so his back had faced the door. Since that fateful night, he'd switched it around so his attention would always be aimed at the door. No one would ever walk up behind him unaware again.

"I'm sorry it turned out this way. Five damn years wasted on a misunderstanding." Jason took a swallow of his drink. "You need to talk to her."

"I have your blessing to date your baby sister? You hated every guy that even looked at her funny."

Jason laughed. "Because that's what big brothers do, man. They put the fear of God in every man for even thinking about touching their sister. But you..." Jason nudged his shoulder. "I was waiting for you to tell me that you wanted her. You had my blessing back then, and you still have it."

Rider felt like he was dreaming. That he'd wake up at any moment and this wouldn't be real. Somehow he'd fallen asleep at his table working too hard on the most important case of his career. Stromberg had been right. He needed to take care of himself and get some rest. This was what happened when he didn't. He created shit in his mind that would never happen.

He brought his hand up to his heart, rubbing.

"You do that a lot. Why?"

Rider's head twitched, realizing that he wasn't dreaming and Jason was sitting on his couch giving him his blessing.

"It's a long story."

Jason shifted on the couch as if finding the most comfortable position he could. "I got some more time before I should go. I want to hear it. Then I want to hear you tell me you're going to talk to Junelle. I need the two people in my life I care about the most to be happy. And right now, both of you are so miserable it makes me want to scream."

"I've changed. I'm sure she's changed. I doubt she wants to hear anything I have to say."

"You won't know until you try. Please. For me."

Rider couldn't deny that plea even though he wanted to.

He'd pushed his best friend away for five years when he didn't have to. He wasn't about to keep making the same idiotic mistakes.

He'd talk to Junelle, and maybe for once in his life, something would go the right way.

3

SHE WISHED her friends a safe drive home—something they all did to each other every time they parted ways—then closed the front door.

Jason was in the kitchen tidying up the mess she and her friends had created. If he was going to go all Suzy Homemaker on her, then that meant he had something on his mind.

"Are you okay?"

He looked up from the rag he'd been dragging around the counter to wipe up the drops of salsa coating the surface. "Yeah, why wouldn't I be?"

She chuckled when he started scrubbing the surface as if it was his life mission to make it shine so hard he'd see his reflection.

"No reason at all."

He stopped his vigorous movements, laughing. "I'm worried about you. What else can I say?"

"Where did you go?" She wanted to start there.

Jason was never one to shy away from anything. Not

even the hard conversations. His gaze never wavered from her. "I visited Rider."

She should've known that's where he'd go. He would want answers that she doubted Rider gave him. Not if he liked living.

"And? Did they find anything out yet?"

Ignoring the real reason he went would be better. If she didn't bring it up, hopefully he wouldn't either.

"No. Forensics could take a while." Jason crossed his arms and leveled a hard glare her way. "You should've told me about those letters. Why didn't you?"

"Because I wanted to pretend they weren't real."

They both knew how overprotective he could be. That reason would be obvious. She hadn't told anyone—not her parents, friends, or Jason—about the letters. Because if she hid them, they didn't exist. At least, that's what she tried to tell herself. No one had ever approached her or sent her anything else, like flowers or chocolate, so it was easy to dismiss the letters.

"They're real, all right." His gaze glided to the sliding glass door where her backyard was.

Yeah, she couldn't pretend any longer. Her poor Molly. Sweet, lovable Molly. Tears rose to the surface again and she had to force them down. She wouldn't break down in front of her brother. Tears were only acceptable in her room where she could bawl her eyes out to her heart's content. Alone. Something she had already done and knew she'd do again before the night was over.

"You know I have to tell Mom and Dad," he added, but his gaze hadn't left the same view.

"I already called Mom earlier. Saved you the trouble."

His attention jerked back to her. "Did you tell them not to cut their vacation short?"

Considering they had saved up for years to take a trip to Italy, no, she had not suggested they come home early. But she had needed to hear her mom's voice. The comfort of it. The soothing words she knew she'd deliver. It helped. For that short moment in time, it had helped the loss of losing her beloved pet.

"They're not leaving. I made them promise."

Jason nodded. "Good. Now I'm not surprised you told them about Molly, but did you mention the letters too?"

Meaning, if she hadn't, he would. Which was what he'd meant with his original comment.

"No, and you won't either. Not while they're in Italy. When they come home, I won't keep it from them. I promise. By that time, this should all be settled."

His eyes widened as if he couldn't believe she said something so ridiculous. Settled? Yeah, that would be wishful thinking on her part. She'd been getting the crude letters for the past three months. Each one escalated a little more sexual, a little more fueled with anger.

Now Molly was gone.

She should've seen the violence coming. The letters should've been a clue the person was losing their patience.

"I hope it's settled by then."

She did too.

"Rider told me the truth." His look intensified the longer they stared at one another. "Everything that happened between you two."

That surprised her. She didn't think Rider would've caved after keeping it between them for five years.

How badly did Jason beat him? His fists could fly when he got riled up. He'd been arrested twice for fighting in a bar. She'd scolded him both times when she had to bail his ass out. Each time had been for sticking up for women being accosted by drunken assholes. So she hadn't reamed him as much as she would've for any other reason.

She glanced at his hands to see the markings that would indicate he'd thrown a few punches. They looked free and clear.

"You could've told me that you were dating him back then."

She scoffed, shaking her head. "No way. You would've flipped a lid. You would've hated it."

"Rider thought the same thing. And I corrected him on that wrong notion. He's one of the best guys in this world. I would never have worried one minute while you were dating him, knowing he was treating you right."

"He cheated on me." So much for being the best guy in the world!

Light laughter filled the space. "You saw him with an arm around a girl. Is that right? That's all."

What more proof had she needed? Why have his arm around a girl to begin with?

She gave a tight dip of her head. More tears were threatening to rise to the surface.

"You know he's always wanted to be a detective. He would've done anything for that chance right away. So when they asked him to do some undercover work, he jumped at it. Unfortunately, that brought him up close with people he didn't want to be close to. Even more unfortunate, you witnessed part of it."

No.

She knew what she saw.

Yet, the truth held strong in Jason's eyes.

She'd lost five years with a man she loved because she never gave him a chance to explain. One he had begged her to give him.

"It's never too late to make amends, June." Then Jason walked past her, touching her shoulder in comfort. He made sure the sliding door was locked. She heard the alarm beep indicating he had set it.

She stood there, trying to process the mistake she'd made so many years ago. After standing for several minutes, she jerked herself out of the stupor she'd been thrust in and got ready for bed herself.

Her townhouse had two bedrooms. She got lucky when she rented it. After renting for two years, the owner wanted to sell and let her buy it for a steal. Literally the sole reason she had been able to afford such a nice townhouse in a great neighborhood.

Until this morning, she had felt safe.

Even with Jason across the hallway, her safety net had been wiped away. She locked her bedroom door, feeling better, but not by much. Considering the police couldn't find how the person broke in, it increased her fears exponentially.

When she curled under the covers, fiddling with her phone, she knew she'd never be brave enough to reach out to Rider.

Not after the accusations she'd thrown in his face.

Hell, he probably didn't even have the same number any longer. Jason had handled sending the list of men who had asked her out, not her.

If he hadn't cheated, which it sounded like he hadn't, then she'd treated him like a scum ball for no reason. There would be no coming back from that.

Just her luck to get Jason's blessings to date his best friend, and the man himself hated her.

Because the fierce frown he'd worn the entire time he'd been here today said he'd developed a true hatred for her.

He'd never forgive her even if she offered an apology.

And he deserved one.

When the time was right, she would give it. But for now, she'd keep it to herself.

"Wee-uh, wee-uh, wee-uh."

Rider looked up from his desk, crumpled a piece of paper, and threw it at Tate who was making annoying emergency services sounds.

"Do you mind?"

Tate caught the paper, grinning like the devil. "Nope. That was your warning call that we're leaving. Get up and out of that chair before I make you."

If he could shout nasty obscenities at his captain for assigning him to work with these two, he would. Except he liked his job and didn't want to get fired.

"You could've said that. It's time to go. Try it, Tate. It's easy."

"What, and miss getting a rise out of you. Not a chance." Then he winked and turned around, expecting Rider to follow him without any further badgering.

And damn it. He did follow right away.

What did he mean by getting a rise out of him? He'd done it on purpose? For what end game? Because Tate didn't bother him as if they were friends or something. Rarely spoke to him unless it was necessary. While Stromberg had become partners—and friends—with Tate, not a whole lot of people liked him. Tate rubbed people the wrong way more times than not.

Rider caught up with Stromberg, who trailed behind Tate to walk with him.

"Don't look so cranky to be working with us again."

"Is he always that annoying?"

Stromberg chuckled. "He must've gotten out of the right side of the bed today. He's pretty chipper this morning. That is a rarity for him."

Ugh. The day couldn't end soon enough. He didn't know if he could deal with both of these guys all day long.

"Trust me. You're going to turn that frown upside down when I tell you where we're going."

"Well, cut the suspense, Stromberg, and spit it out."

"Your girlfriend's house."

His heart skipped a beat. Several, actually. In rapid succession. He rubbed his chest, hoping to dispel the sudden pain and erratic pounding.

Stromberg stopped walking, putting a hand on his shoulder, which forced him to stop as well. "Yo, dude, nothing bad happened to her. That's not what I meant."

Funny enough, his mind hadn't veered to something bad had happened. But more along the lines of hearing her being called his girlfriend.

If only.

Even his dreams wouldn't give him that satisfaction.

He forced himself to drop his hand. "Then why are we going there?"

"A neighbor at the end of the street was doing some recording. You know how everyone is posting shit on social media these days. He caught some weirdo in a car in the background. He heard about Molly and brought it over to her this morning. The brother called. So that's why we're heading there. Nothing nefarious. I promise."

"She's not my girlfriend." Then he walked away before he blurted anything else out.

Why hadn't Jason called him? Which one of these buffoons had he reached out to?

He was silent in the backseat while Stromberg drove and Tate lounged in the front passenger seat. They made it to Junelle's house in short time and he thought he'd composed himself enough. But he hadn't. Not even close. His anger stayed with him while they walked to the front door.

Despite the nice conversation he had with Jason last night, nothing felt better. Rider still wanted to ignore his best friend and walk the other way. Five years of solitude from the one you loved would do that to a person.

Tate knocked on the door. Junelle answered it. They made eye contact, but it was so brief, he couldn't gauge what she was thinking.

"Come on in. I have coffee if you'd like a cup."

"I'd love one, thank you," Stromberg said in a cordial tone as if they were coming over for a simple visit. Nothing about this damn case was simple. Tate even accepted a cup.

He grumbled no thanks and left it at that. She looked like he'd slapped her, and he regretted his bad attitude. He didn't want to be angry, especially not at her. Hurting her was the last thing he wanted to do, even if she had crushed his heart into tiny pieces.

"So you called about a video?" Tate asked.

Wait? She called, or Jason called? Because it made a difference to him. It had bothered him the entire ride why Jason hadn't called him. But if it had been Junelle, then he understood. No harm done.

"Yes."

"Where's your brother?" Stromberg asked, and Rider was, once again, grateful these two were here to ask questions he couldn't get past his lips.

"In the shower. He'll be down soon. Crap." She looked

around the kitchen, then winced. "I left my phone upstairs. I'll be right back."

As soon as she left the room, he pounced. "Stromberg, you said Jason called you."

Stromberg flinched at the venom in his voice. "Tate took the call. I assumed it was the brother."

Tate grinned, an evil one that said Rider was going to have a day from hell working with him. "No, it was Junelle who called."

Great.

Another misunderstanding, and this time, this one sent his anxiety through the roof. After last night, he had thought he'd been on better terms with Jason. Back to maybe being friends again after such a long break. Then one sentence had tattered those hopes.

He'd worried for no damn reason because Jason hadn't been the one to call.

"Does that hurt your feelings she called me and not you?"

He took a step toward Tate. Stromberg had to block him. Then Stromberg hissed at his partner, "What are you doing, asshole?"

"Hey, you pussyfooting around him isn't doing shit. You want him out of his shell, I'm bringing him out, jackass."

Well, Rider couldn't disagree with that. Tate was sure bringing out the fury like no one else could. But Tate might not like how he reacted to whatever idiotic thing he did next.

Stromberg chuckled, sweeping his hands toward Rider though kept his gaze on Tate. "By all means, asshole, keep pissing him off. He's bound to knock you on your ass."

Tate widened his grin. "As my partner, jackass, you'll step in to help me."

Then the two were laughing it up as if they'd shared the world's greatest joke with each other. Rider was so confused, he lost some of the ire Tate had created.

"So you're purposely trying to piss me off to get a reaction?" he asked to make sure he understood what was going on.

Tate bobbed his head up and down as a wily smile graced his lips. "You haven't been yourself, Rider. Everyone knows it and hates it. I care because Stromberg cares. If I can help, I will. You've wanted to hit me twice now. A different emotion than just indifference, which means I'm doing something right."

He rubbed his chest, hating how much Tate's words affected him.

"Why has he been acting indifferent?"

Their attention turned to the threshold of the kitchen where Jason stood, his hair still wet. Jason pointed at him. "You're doing it again. Rubbing your chest. You never did explain last night why you do that."

"He does do that a lot, you're right," Tate noted.

"Shut up, Tate," he grumbled.

"Hey," Tate started.

"Please. Shut it," he growled. Maybe it was the added please that had Tate clamping his mouth shut.

He dropped his hand from his chest. He had to stop doing that.

"I don't want to talk about it."

The focused gleam in Jason's eyes said Rider wouldn't be getting out of it altogether. He'd have to spill his guts sooner or later.

"Found it!" Junelle said cheerfully, rejoining them. She had either added the peppiness to erase the tension in the air, or she hadn't heard a word of the exchange and was truly happy. He found that doubtful, with everything that was going on.

Either way, Rider was glad she returned. He never wanted to talk about how he'd let himself get stabbed. How useless he'd been when someone important to Stromberg had been in danger.

"Here you go." She set her phone on the counter, hit the screen, and stepped back.

All three of them crowded the space to watch the video.

One man was front and center, talking about certain stretches one should do before working out, especially running. Rider assumed he was the neighbor who'd delivered the video. One minute into his speech, an old beat-up car that had to be at least thirty years old rolled into the frame. The man stared straight ahead, not paying attention to anyone but the road ahead of him.

Rider took the lead, stopping the video and rewinding. It took three times watching it to confirm why the neighbor thought this video would be useful.

The man had blood on his cheek. When he zoomed in, he could even see spatters of blood on his clothes. As if he had murdered someone—like a furry someone—in a fit of rage. Rider was surprised the gentleman even noticed the blood, because one had to zoom in to see it. Again, he assumed the guy was particular about his videos before he uploaded them for the whole world to see.

"It's hard to make out his full details. It's a side view of him," Tate commented.

True. That was disappointing.

But the video managed to get the last three digits of his license plate. He could work with three digits. And an old beater of a car. Shouldn't be too hard to find the owner. Not if he made it his life's mission to do so.

"We'll get him." He gritted his teeth to hold the rage he felt simmering to the surface. He watched the video again, then backed away from it before he lost control and smashed the phone.

"Can you please send me that video?" He should've looked at Junelle when he asked, but he didn't have the courage. Not yet. The fury was building inside. That someone thought they could terrorize her. Kill her pet. Make her feel—well, Rider didn't know how she felt, but he knew it wasn't good.

When she didn't respond, he looked at her.

She was on the verge of tears, and he hated himself for being the one to make her cry.

His hand reached up to his chest and rubbed. Even harder than he had before.

4

THOSE DUMB TEARS were making their way back to the surface, and she loathed showing that weakness. She didn't want to cry in front of any of these men, especially Rider and her brother. She'd already bawled uncontrollably last night in bed. It had created a huge headache and she had trouble sleeping. She didn't want another headache. Because she knew if the tears started again, they wouldn't stop for a long time.

But the way Rider sounded so confident, so filled with rage on her behalf, hit her. Right in the heart where she had built a strong, impenetrable wall to keep people out. Without even trying, Rider was knocking that wall down bit by bit.

"Yes, of course, I'll send it to you right now." She shook her head, hoping the tears would remain inside, and picked up her phone. She went to her contacts and froze. "I don't have your number."

At least, she wasn't sure if his number was the same from five years ago. She had never had the courage to delete it. And she wasn't about to admit that.

Nor would she confess she'd kept the necklace he'd given her for her twenty-second birthday. Two hearts intertwined. She'd dug it out of her jewelry box last night and put it back on. It currently hid underneath her shirt.

Rider cleared his throat, then shoved his hand in his back pocket, producing his wallet. Then he pulled out a card and set it on the counter. It hurt how he took care to keep his distance from her.

She only had herself to blame.

A quick glance at the number on the card said he hadn't changed it. She could've called or texted him at any point in the past five years. Including last night to beg for forgiveness.

All night she had tossed and turned, pondering the life she could've had. If she had given him a chance to explain...

Five years...

Five dreadful years apart.

Knowing he hadn't broken the bond between them, that he never cheated on her—it brought all those feelings she had pushed aside back to the surface.

She loved Rider.

She always would.

By his solemn expression and the way he could never meet her eyes, she knew he had stopped loving her a long time ago.

She pretended to add his number and then sent the video.

"Do you think you can find out who that guy is?" Jason asked.

"I will." Rider sounded so, so confident in the matter.

"But it could take time. There isn't a lot to go on," Detective Powell added. Junelle didn't miss the way he glared at Rider as if admonishing him for making a promise.

"I saw there is a security system," Rider noted, looking at Jason. "But you need to set up security cameras outside. One on the front door and one on the back door. Make sure you change the locks as well."

Jason gave him a sharp nod. "I'll get it done today."

She hated to think her life would be under a microscope, but if it would help catch this creep, then she was all for it.

"Where do you work, Junelle?" Rider still wouldn't look her in the eye. For a simple question too.

He knew she had gone to college and received a Fine Arts degree. But since he hadn't been around for her actual graduation or anything thereafter, he had no idea what she'd focused on. Again, all her fault.

"I work at one of the theaters on Broadway. Well, off-Broadway. I work on props and whatnot."

She'd loved drawing and painting since she could remember. Her parents had given in when she asked them nonstop if she could draw on her walls. It went from simple drawings to artistically challenging images where she then painted everything. Her room still had it all up on the walls at her parents' house. She was so proud of that. She had yet to do anything like that in her own home. One day though, she would.

"How's the security there?"

"Like shit," Jason answered Rider's question before she could. "Sure, during performances that place is locked down, but not during off hours. The other day, she told me how her co-worker had money stolen from her wallet."

"No doubt by another employee," she interjected.

"That backdoor is never locked from the street. It should be. Yeah, sure, another employee could've nabbed the money, but someone also could've strolled in without anyone knowing."

"Where have all the letters been delivered?" Tate asked.

"Here." She shivered thinking about every time she opened her front door and another sat waiting on the top step. They never had a return address attached to it, so she knew whoever left them was doing it on their own. Plus, she never found any in her mailbox. Always on her doorstep. One had even been stuck under the door as if the person tried to shove it underneath and failed.

"So, as far as we know, nothing has happened at her workplace," Tate continued.

"We can't discredit anything," Rider said. His lips were so straight, and his words so low, she swore he was gritting his teeth as he said it. Even a muscle or two jumped in his cheek. "Please be aware of your surroundings and try not to be alone in any part of the building while you're there."

"I can do that."

She stared at him so hard, as if she could force him with the power of her eyes to look at her. He didn't twitch in the slightest.

"I have the next few days off. I...needed some time off." She didn't need to explain why.

"I also took the next few days off. She won't be alone at home." Jason's lips turned down. "I don't like to think of you by yourself at work either."

"I won't be. Tawney knows everything." Jason knew that because she was one of the friends who had come over last night. "She'll be by my side at work. I know she won't have a problem with that."

Jason seemed satisfied by that answer. "Well, maybe she should show you a few of the defensive moves she knows so well. I can teach you how to throw a proper punch, but she could give you pointers as well."

What a great idea! Tawney knew a few different forms of martial arts: Judo, karate, Jiu-Jitsu to name a few. She went to a local gym not far from where they worked at least four nights a week. She loved keeping in shape.

"I'll join her at the gym." It wasn't easy getting a membership there as they were particular about who joined, but one word from Tawney and she knew she wouldn't have a problem.

"Good. Do that."

"A plan. I love plans," Detective Stromberg said with a cheeriness nobody else had displayed. "We'll leave you two be. Don't hesitate to call if anything else happens or you think of something else we need to know."

She thanked them for coming and walked them to the door. Jason said his goodbyes in the kitchen. She knew he would scrounge for breakfast as he hadn't eaten yet. Rider was the last to exit the door. She wasn't sure if that was intentional or not, but she couldn't pass up this opportunity. Before he could walk out, she reached out and touched his shoulder.

He stiffened, causing her to jerk her hand back. But he turned around, and that's all she'd wanted. His attention for once.

The power of his gaze nearly knocked her on her ass. So full of hurt and sorrow. But none of the desire he'd had for her five years ago.

"Thank you for coming."

That was *not* what she wanted to say, but it was a good place to start.

"You're welcome." He didn't smile, not even in his crystal-blue eyes. Had he even meant the polite comment?

"Jason told me..." She paused, unsure how to frame it. "He told me about his visit with you last night."

There. That should give him a clue about what she was alluding to.

He nodded. "Okay."

Okay?

That's it?

It crushed her that she'd ruined the best thing to ever happen to her. He didn't even have anything left inside him to forgive her. Again, all her fault.

"I'm sorry, Rider. That I never gave you the chance to explain anything. I'm sorry I accused you of doing something you didn't. Can you forgive me?"

If he wouldn't give his forgiveness on his own, then she'd have to ask for one. Plead, if necessary.

He gave her another nod, this one tight and rigid. "Okay."

She wanted to scream at his one-worded responses.

He swallowed hard, continuing. "It's in the past. There's no need to rehash any of it. Let's move on."

She'd love the sound of that if it meant they could move on together. At least form a friendship again. The one thing she had missed in the last five years, besides his wondrous touch, was his undying support and friendship. He had been her friend before he had ever been her boyfriend.

"So you don't hate me?"

His expression never wavered from the hard rigid lines. Then his hand reached up and rubbed his chest.

"I could never hate you, June Bug."

Then he turned and jaunted down the steps before she could reply. As if he had nothing else to say to her. They made amends—kind of—but there would be no rekindling of any kind of relationship, even one where they were friends.

Yet...

He'd called her June Bug.

With that sweet nickname ringing in her ears, she held on to a small ounce of hope they could be friends one day.

Nooooooooo!

What was that damn brother doing?

He couldn't set up security cameras. That would make it impossible for him to get close again. For him to leave another important message to her. She needed to know how upset she made him. How her lack of respect and ignoring him caused him undue pain.

His car scrolled past with normal speed despite the urge to put his foot on the brakes a little.

This was no doubt the cops' fault. Telling them to spruce up security.

Ha! As if that would keep him out.

It might make his mission harder, but it wouldn't stop him.

The drive home was a blur. He didn't remember a moment of it, from getting to point A to point B. All his mind could focus on was the obstacle they had thrown in his face. But he'd find a workaround no matter what.

After showering, he put on his uniform and left for work. People greeted him as he entered the building. Of course, he returned the sentiment with a smile. No one would ever know the turmoil going on inside him. All these people thought they were the best actors and actresses in the world, but they fell short by a mile.

He was the best performer there ever was.

"Hey, Junelle took a few days off. Someone killed her dog. Can you believe it?"

The shock morphed so easily in his features. The disgust as well. His co-worker, Paul, shared the same look. "That's horrible. Who would do such a thing?"

Honestly, he was curious about that. What compelled other people to hurt animals? He would've never seen himself as an animal killer, but it had happened. He couldn't deny it. While he didn't lose sleep over it, he felt a small morsel of regret. The dog hadn't done anything to him but be kind. A trait Junelle had never displayed toward him. She didn't deserve his respect, but her dog had. So yeah, he held a small amount of remorse for his actions.

"A damn psycho, that's who. No one in their right mind hurts animals."

A tingling sensation went up his spine.

The same feeling he got when Junelle ignored him. When people didn't give him the credit he deserved.

"I hope she's okay."

He'd ignore this imbecile's words for now. Plus, he had a part to play. The concerned co-worker over another person's misfortune.

"Yeah, I guess. She's distraught. Her dog was killed." Paul rolled his eyes as if he couldn't believe he'd said such a thing.

The tingling increased to the point his stomach clenched, indicating he was on the verge of throwing up. He'd never embarrass himself in front of this asshole.

"Just terrible. So, so terrible." Then he smiled. "I have to make my rounds. See ya, Paul."

Then he turned around before he unleashed the rage

building in his system. His first stop was the bathroom where he proceeded to lose his stomach contents.

Why did people have to treat him with such disrespect? Rolling his eyes? Like he had said something stupid.

He wasn't stupid, even if his father had uttered that phrase a time or two growing up.

When he exited the stall, one of the performers was washing his hands. He made sure to use a sink a distance away from him, especially when he looked at him like he carried a contagious disease. He took no offense to it. The people who commanded the stage day in and day out couldn't afford to get sick.

"Not sick, man. I promise." He touched his stomach, faking a grimace that appeared real. "Do not eat the tacos at the end of the block. That vendor needs to lose his license for selling food. Seriously."

The performer offered a sympathetic smile. "Thanks for the advice. They smelled delicious on my way in. I was going to grab one."

"Walk the other way."

They laughed together.

"Thanks for the heads-up."

Then he was alone in the bathroom.

People could be so gullible.

People could be so mean.

Sometimes, the mean ones needed to learn a lesson in etiquette.

5

HE DIDN'T LOOK up when a shadow loomed over him. There was no need to as it was either Tate or Stromberg, and he didn't need either of them bugging him. Who cared the captain forced him to work with them. It didn't mean he'd make it easy on anyone. Maybe they'd get the hint he worked better alone—at least, these days he did. He never had a problem tackling a case with other people before he'd been injured. But now...

Now he was a failure. No one should *want* to work with him.

"Find anything yet?"

But that was the thing about those two. They didn't give up or give in. Ever.

Rider glanced at Stromberg with a sharp shake of his head. He'd been combing the DMV database for the last two hours, coming up empty. He had the last three digits to the license plate, but there were also a lot of New York residents. It could take him longer than he wanted. But damn it. He'd find the bastard who wanted to hurt Junelle.

"We're going to grab some lunch. Let's go."

He gave Stromberg another sharp shake of his head.

"You need to eat."

Yeah, he did. But not with them.

When his gaze remained on the screen, ignoring Stromberg's looming presence, the man got the hint and walked away. A low, audible breath released.

While deep down he could appreciate his friends' concern and wanting to help pull him out of his rut, he didn't want their help. He didn't want them to care so much. The longer he maintained his distance, the more they'd get the idea he would never cave in.

His eyes blurred every now and again as he scrolled through the system, looking for his perp. His stomach even took the opportunity to grumble at him.

Okay, so he was hungry. He didn't bring a lunch, but he could grab a bag of chips from the vending machine in a few minutes. By the time those two returned, he would have stuffed his belly—albeit not decently—but he'd be ready for whatever they made him do. While he wanted to keep his entire focus on Junelle's case, he had a dozen more that also needed his attention. That didn't take into account Tate and Stromberg's cases either. Provided he was supposed to help them since he was stuck working with them.

Their only lead with Junelle's case was her car. Molly's autopsy had revealed nothing helpful. Multiple stab wounds that led to severe blood loss. Official cause of death. No helpful evidence had been found on or around the body. No forced entry had been detected and no useful prints around the house either. Forensics was still working on the letters, but as of yet, no viable prints—other than Junelle's—had been found. So he'd sit at his desk all day combing through the DMV until he found something. He had to!

Another shadow loomed over him. It hadn't been more

than ten minutes since Stromberg left. They couldn't have eaten that fast and returned already. Which meant they hadn't left yet and he wanted to try one more time to convince him to join them.

"Piss off."

The startled squeak at his side had him lifting his gaze.

Junelle stood clutching her purse in her hands with a desolate, hurt expression in her glistening emerald eyes.

Shit.

He hadn't meant to take his annoyance out on her.

Damn! He missed the way her eyes used to light up at seeing him. So bright and beautiful and sparkling like a magnificent gem. He'd decided emeralds were his favorite every time he looked into her eyes. Now all he saw was disgust. Shadows lingering in the depths. And dullness. Nothing but a dull, dreary desert land.

And he was staring, instead of apologizing for acting like a jackass.

"I'm sorry. I thought you were someone else."

Even though she motioned she understood, as if accepting his half-ass apology, the hurt remained.

His gaze darted around her, his brows furrowing low. "Where's Jason? Is everything okay?"

"Yes, of course." Her hands twisted the strap, her knuckles turning white. "He dropped me off. He had a work thing he had to attend to, and I told him I wouldn't mind stopping by to see you."

A spark of hope lit up her green eyes, displaying a flicker of beauty. He hated seeing it. He'd accepted her apology and had forgiven her for her part in their breakup. It hadn't been that difficult. Staying mad at Junelle was impossible. Especially when he still loved her so much. He doubted he'd ever stop loving her, no matter what she might do to him.

But there was no chance they'd ever get together again. He'd risked a lot back then to be with her. His friendship with Jason. His heart. It all had come crumbling down around him when she walked away. He was afraid to give her that power again. She didn't have faith in him, not enough trust. What would she do if another misunderstanding occurred? Blame him again without giving him a chance to explain?

Why was his addled brain even thinking such scenarios? She deserved better than someone like him—an utter failure.

He gestured toward the chair near his desk. "Have a seat." He had no choice but to offer her one. If Jason had dropped her off, he was stuck with her for the time being.

She sat down, shoving her hands in her lap and avoiding eye contact. It gave him time to stare when he knew he shouldn't. Dwelling on her, hoping for things that weren't possible, was torturing himself.

Then he saw it.

The necklace he'd given her for her birthday. The moment their relationship went from friendship to so much more. He couldn't believe she kept it. Had she worn it the entire time they'd been apart? Or did she just start wearing it now? What did it mean that she was wearing it?

Her gaze finally lifted, and he got lost in her enchanting green eyes.

"What are you working on?"

This was what they were reduced to? Idle chit-chat.

Yesterday, she couldn't stand to look at him. Now she looked at him as if she wanted to pick up right where they left off five years ago.

Why in the hell couldn't she have given him the chance

to explain back then? Why did they have to lose so much time together?

Anger built as the questions swirled through his mind.

So, okay, maybe he hadn't forgiven her yet.

It pissed him off she let her brother explain everything and believed it without incident. But him—he couldn't get one word in.

Not that they had exchanged the word love back then, but he'd sensed it in her. At least, he had thought she loved him. But how could she have? She walked away without arguing with him. Without questioning him. Without even giving him a chance to explain.

"Or I can sit here and let you work until Jason returns. I won't bother you."

Damn it!

He was being an asshole again. He might not give a shit acting that way with other people, but it gutted him to do it to Junelle. It didn't matter if he still held a hint of anger toward her, he didn't want to hurt her in return.

"I've been trying to find the full license plate and registration for the car in that video. No luck yet."

"But you think you will?"

"I will."

They may never be a couple ever again, but he'd die before he let someone hurt her. He would not rest until he found this bastard.

"I know you said we should leave the past in the past." She bit her bottom lip, then swiped her tongue across it. "But I sense you hate me. I don't blame you at all. I thought the worst of you when it wasn't even close to the truth, and I want to know how I can make this right between us. I don't want you hating me."

"I don't hate you." God, never. He could never hate her.

"The scowl on your face says you do."

That was a permanent expression he wore. It had nothing to do with her. He couldn't remember the last time he laughed or even offered a genuine smile. Not that he'd divulge any of that to her.

"I mean it when I say I don't hate you. I could never." He forced his entire body to relax and portray a more gentle posture. "I'm sad we lost so many years together. I'm mad that you never gave me a chance to explain. I'm...I'm a different person than I was back then. But I do forgive you, Junelle. I want to move on from that."

"Okay, I won't bring it up again. I'm sorry. I should've known you'd never do something like that."

Yeah, well, he thought she would've known too. But it was done and over with. If they kept on this conversation, he couldn't say how he'd react.

"Rider, my favorite detective!"

He suppressed a groan, but twisted to watch as Bri approached his desk carrying a Tupperware container. Out of the corner of his eye, he saw Junelle frown and narrow her gaze at Bri. Jealous, perhaps? One could hope.

No!

He didn't want her to be jealous. He didn't want her thinking anything could happen again between them. How could he trust her to not hurt him again?

And the even better question, how could she trust him to keep her safe? She should stay far away from him for her own good.

"You look handsome today."

He rolled his eyes at Bri's odd compliment, noting Junelle's flashing with fire. More jealousy? A weird sensation hit his heart.

His hand reached up and started rubbing over the spot to remove it.

He was not going down that path again with her. Just to get his heart crushed once more when she mistook his actions for something they weren't. She could take her jealousy and...suffer in it.

The odd sensation turned into an aching pain as that nasty thought rolled through his mind, despising himself for even thinking such a thing. He started rubbing his chest more vigorously.

Bri noticed Junelle sitting by him, wincing. "I'm sorry. I didn't realize you were in the middle of something. I promise I won't be long. I'm dropping off some cookies. I hope whatever issue you're having isn't serious. You have one of the best detectives on your case."

"Thank you. I know that."

The sharp bite of Junelle's words had a chuckle rising from his chest and escaping.

All three froze at the sound. Even his hand on his chest stopped moving.

"Did you just laugh?" Bri looked amazed he'd uttered such a melodic sound. He hadn't done so in so long.

"No."

"Oh my gosh!" Junelle admonished, tapping his shoulder with flare, chuckling herself. "We both heard it. You did."

His hand dropped from his chest as his gaze glided to the spot she had touched. Such a brief touch, but enough to have his heart pitter-pattering the way it used to when they were together.

"Okay, fine. A short chuckle came out. I wouldn't call it a laugh. I mean, you don't even know me anymore to say I'm a good detective."

The second the words came out, he wanted to take them back. Junelle's charming expression fell into the deep despair she'd walked in with.

"I'm sor—"

"I know when you put your mind to something," Junelle said, cutting off his apology, "you're a force to be reckoned with. Therefore, that could only mean you're one of the best."

Ugh. No one to blame but herself for the animosity between them. If only...

Well, there was no use wallowing in regrets. She had to make him forgive her. Somehow. Some way. Even if they'd never be a couple again, she wouldn't say no to friendship. She'd missed him so much she couldn't even find the right words to describe it. Perhaps that intense emotion she'd experienced the last five years should've been clue enough that deep down she knew he would never treat her with such disrespect. If her devastated mind had listened to her tattered heart back then, life could have been so different. But she'd been too distraught to see what she should've known to be true.

"I thought I was interrupting you with a work thing, but I'm starting to get the sense you two know each other."

Junelle drew her gaze away from Rider and at the woman he'd called Bri. She'd forgotten she was standing there. How could she have? The woman was someone close to Rider. The interaction thus far told her so. His girlfriend? If that was the case, she had no luck with him. Bri was beautiful with her dark-brown, nearly black hair and the most arresting amber-colored eyes she'd ever seen.

"He's best friends with my brother."

"Used to be," Rider muttered.

She jerked her gaze back at him. "You are."

He had to be. She needed him back in her life, and if that meant through Jason, she'd take it.

Rider huffed, then turned his full attention to Bri. "How can I help you?"

"You don't have to look so happy to see me," Bri teased, swiping a lock of hair behind her ear.

His scowl increased. What did the woman want, and how did she know Rider? She needed those two questions answered. Now.

"Again, how can I—"

The woman's eyes filled with water, surprising Rider into silence. Junelle shared the sentiment. What game was this woman playing?

"Shit, Bri. Don't cry. What the hell?" He stood up, reached out, then stopped himself before touching her. "What's going on?"

"Wyatt told me you have to work with him and Tate for a while. He comes home every day and never tells me anything good about you."

Who was Wyatt? Could that be Detective Stromberg? And the rest of the woman's comments confused her.

"I'm fine. You all need to stop worrying."

Bri swiped a tear away. "You're not fine. And it's all my fault." She thrust out the container toward him. "I made you cookies. Not that it will make up for what I did."

Rider's jaw dropped for a second before he shook his head. "You did nothing wrong, Bri. Shit." He closed his eyes, his jaw clenching for the longest time before he popped them back open. "If anyone should be sorry, it's me. I failed you."

"If I didn't have a psycho after me, you would've never been in my apartment. You would've never been hurt."

Rider had been hurt?

Junelle's heart rate sped up.

How badly?

She wanted to jump into the conversation and ask so many questions, but she remained silent, sensing one wrong word and the situation would turn volatile.

Rider brought his hand up, rubbing over his heart again. He did that so much. Jason had commented on it, but had no reason for it since Rider wouldn't say why. Now she really wanted to know.

"Thank you for the cookies." Rider took the container, though his other hand still remained on his chest.

"What can I do to make things right?"

The container hit his desk with a light thud as he shook his head at Bri. "You didn't do anything wrong. I don't know what else to say."

Then Bri flung her arms around Rider, and it took all of Junelle's control to hold herself back and not pry her arms off him.

Rider stiffened and didn't return the hug.

"What is going on here?"

Junelle turned her attention to Detective Stromberg, who looked very surprised but with a slight glint of anger. The woman still clung to Rider, who looked so uncomfortable she was losing her control to hold herself back.

"I'm trying to show Rider he has so many people who love him."

"Briella..." Stromberg said with quiet patience, "let the man go before he explodes. Seriously."

If anything, she tightened her hold. Rider groaned as if in pain.

"Tell me you forgive yourself and I'll let go. I have it all wrong. You don't hate me for what happened. You hate yourself."

Forgive himself? Junelle was so confused.

"Briella," Stromberg snapped this time. "Let him go. I hate to have to punch the man for touching you."

That garnered another chuckle out of Rider, and Junelle loved hearing the sound. She sensed he hadn't laughed in a long time.

"Oh, he laughed again." Bri squeezed him tighter.

Then, to Junelle's astonishment, Rider's one arm reached up and hugged her back. "Please let me go before Stromberg beats the living shit out of me. I deserve it, but I have an important case that needs my attention. I don't have the time to recuperate from injuries."

Bri lifted her head, then cupped his cheek. "That's where you're wrong. You do not deserve a beating. It's not your fault. You need to forgive yourself."

His expression grew dangerous in the blink of an eye, and even Junelle flinched by the sudden change. One minute Bri was touching him, the next he had shoved her away. Stromberg stepped closer, sweeping his arms around her.

"A madman broke into your apartment, attacked you, and I didn't do shit!" Rider yelled. "I let it happen. He nearly killed me, and every damn day I wish he had!"

The entire room fell silent at his confession.

Bri looked guilty for forcing it out of him. Stromberg looked ready to beat the hell out of him for pushing Bri. And she wanted to hug him like the other woman had. To take his pain away.

She'd almost lost him and she hadn't even known about it.

Rider turned his dark gaze upon her. "I should be the last one working on your case. I can't protect you. I couldn't even protect Bri."

Then she watched in horror as he left. She stood up to follow him, but her feet wouldn't move.

Stromberg made eye contact with her briefly, then turned his full attention to Bri.

She stopped him from speaking first. "I know, I made a mistake. I rushed him. I shouldn't have pushed him so hard. But you said Tate was and...I'm sorry."

"You were trying to help. I get it, Briella baby. I do. It's not your fault he reacted that way."

"It sure feels like it." Bri turned to her. "Don't listen to him. He's one of the best detectives, truly."

"Okay. Let me handle this." Stromberg pushed Bri behind him, then met her stare head-on. "I imagine you don't even know what all of this was about. I don't know the history between you two, but I sense there is one."

Junelle felt on the verge of tears again. "There is. And it's my fault things went sour between us. Can you tell me what happened? How he almost...died?" She couldn't even comprehend he'd been hurt.

"Briella's sister was murdered. I couldn't solve it. A year later, he tried to strike again and kill Briella. I needed Rider to help me protect her, take her home. That's the day the killer made a move. Stabbed Rider twice. Once in the shoulder, once near the heart. He was very close to death. While I don't hold it against him that he couldn't protect her, he blames himself."

"So that's why he rubs his chest so much." It all made sense now.

"I imagine so. He's not getting off your case. I can promise you that."

"Even if he wants to?"

Because she didn't know how to fight this new Rider. The old Rider she knew she could handle. She knew how to act with him. What methods worked and what didn't. This man....he was a stranger to her.

Stromberg grinned. "He doesn't want to, no matter what he said. He's acting like a child right now. A scared, helpless child." He brushed Bri's back, smiling even wider. "I think you were right trying to hug him. Everyone's been keeping their distance when we should've been smothering him." Then he turned that full-watt smile back Junelle's way. "I think the next hug should be from you."

She wanted it to be.

But she didn't think she'd have the courage to do it. She rejected him years ago. If he did the same thing in return, she would never survive it.

6

HIS SHIFT HAD BEEN BORING. Nothing ever happened, and when Junelle wasn't in the building, there wasn't much to look forward to. That didn't mean he skirted on his duties. He kept up appearances, keeping a vigil eye out, being friendly, and letting no one know how her absence ate him up inside.

That asshole Paul gave him funny looks at times, despite the genial smile on his face. So when his shift ended, coincidentally the same time as Paul's, he followed him. To the grocery store. Then to the bank. To his home where he lived alone.

Charles needed to be fed, so he took a break in his observations and went home, feeding him. He even gave him a few belly rubs before getting his things together.

Duct tape because it was useful in so many ways. He even kept a roll in his car for emergencies. One never knew when one might need it.

A change of clothes. Things could get so messy when handling a knife, he needed another set in case he got blood on them.

His knife, of course. He'd gotten it for Christmas one year from his father. One of the rare gifts his father had ever given him. Though it had been meant for him to use on a hunting trip. One he failed to deliver in his father's expectations. He didn't want to shoot a deer and then gut it. It had been another disappointment in a long line of disappointments he had dished out. But he had kept the knife.

He delivered a few more rubs on Charles's back, then left, leaving a light on. Maybe people would think he was home. Even left the TV on for good measure. Plus, Charles could watch whatever was on—he hadn't bothered to look.

By the time he returned to Paul's house, supper had passed, night had descended, and his fingers were itching to do something he shouldn't love. But oh, he relished teaching people a lesson.

Just like Junelle's house had been easy to break into, Paul's gave him no issues either. The TV was on—the volume up high—in the living room. Though when he peeked inside, the room was empty. He heard the toilet flush. A bathroom break. Good. Paul would be less likely to piss himself when he learned he wasn't alone.

He'd done that before. Lost his bladder from being so scared. It had increased the beating his father had doled out. Despite telling himself repeatedly to hold it in, don't let his father witness such weakness, he could never manage to do so. He hoped Paul did the same, even with his bathroom break. That the fear would be too much for him to handle. Then he wouldn't be the only one who had pissed himself in fear.

Stepping to the side of the threshold of the hallway, he waited patiently for Paul to return to his seat. The curtains were closed in the living room, which made things so much easier for him. No one to witness what he was about to do.

Paul walked right past him, not even sensing he stood right there. He could be light on his feet when he wanted to be. He rushed up behind him before Paul could sit down, pressing the knife to his back. Paul stiffened.

"On your knees. Now," he whispered.

Maybe it was the way he said it so confidently. Or maybe it was the way he pushed the knife into his back, no doubt breaking the skin. Paul cried out in pain, indicating something hurt. But he complied without arguing.

"Hands behind your back."

Didn't hesitate there either.

He took his trusty duct tape and wrapped his hands together without any fuss. Then he slapped a piece over his mouth before stepping in front of him.

Paul's eyes widened in surprise when he recognized him. Though he wasn't able to scream or ask why he had broken in. What were his intentions? Not that he would've answered any of his questions. He was the one in charge. Not Paul.

"I want you to know that I didn't mean to kill Molly."

Paul's eyes enlarged even more, which made him laugh, thinking it wasn't possible for that to happen. But he reveled in the knowledge that Paul knew who had hurt Junelle's pet.

"It was an accident. I do regret it."

Then he went on his knees as well so he could look at Paul eye level. "But I want you to know, I'm not going to regret this. I didn't appreciate how you treated me today, and I've decided I have to teach you a lesson on how to treat others. If I don't do it, who will?"

Paul mumbled as if he'd hear whatever nonsense he was trying to say. He didn't care what Paul had to say.

"Thank you for making this so easy. Sometimes I don't mind a good fight, but I wasn't in the mood for that tonight."

The knife penetrated deep into Paul's gut with one swift movement. More muffled sounds erupted from Paul as he toppled over from the injury. But he didn't stop there. He didn't hold back. He showed no mercy as he taught Paul a lesson he'd never forget.

HE HAD NEVER BEEN one to run away from a problem. Even when things got tough, like when his mom got cancer. They'd all battled through that together, so positive she'd beat it. He had been by her side through the whole ordeal. When she passed, losing the fight that he still couldn't believe she lost, he then switched to be by his dad's side, keeping him from losing himself. At least he tried to while also trying to hold himself together. It had been a hard row to hoe.

But this was the first time he'd run away with his tail between his legs.

Everyone standing there trying to tell him he hadn't done anything wrong. He couldn't stand it.

He was the reason Bri had to fight back.

He was the reason she had to kill that psycho.

He was the reason she nearly died.

Stromberg should hate him.

Bri should despise him.

And Junelle should never trust him with her life.

He'd turned his phone off the moment he stepped outside the precinct. It didn't matter who called him, he had no intention of speaking to anyone. At first, he roamed around the city, going nowhere in particular. He tried to clear his mind of everything. Yet, it all swirled around, infecting him like a savage disease, hellbent on killing him.

After a while his feet hurt from all the walking. Not once had it occurred to him to sit down and relax. Because if he did, his brain would work even harder to send him down the rabbit hole he was trying to avoid.

Instead of calling for a ride or grabbing the subway, he walked all the way home. By the time he made it, he was ready to die from exhaustion. On autopilot, he locked his door then made his way to his room. He de-robed right there, letting the clothes fall to the ground without a care, and jumped into the shower. For the longest time he let the water flow over him. First super-hot, then turning cold he had stood there so long. By the time he realized he'd wasted ample opportunity to wash himself, he was forced to do so in the coldness.

Even the steam had died down, not requiring him to wipe it away from the mirror. He stared at himself, looking at every tiny detail until everything blurred.

He failed.

He failed to protect Bri.

And now another person's life—not just any person—was on the line, and he feared he'd fail again. If he stepped away, there was no chance of failure. At least on his part.

With that knowledge securely planted, he knew he made the right decision. Walking away was the only thing he could do. If the captain had a problem with him removing himself from the case, then he'd hand in his badge. He couldn't be around Junelle and risk her life.

She could die because of him.

He rubbed his bristled chin, deciding he needed to trim his beard some. He'd let it get too thick the last few days. He didn't like it like that.

Once done, he got dressed and sat on his couch. Instead of turning his phone back on, he stared at it. Because once he called his captain, it was a done deal. He couldn't change his mind. Hell, his captain could be one of the people who called him. No doubt wondering why he left work during the middle of the day without telling him.

It didn't matter if his captain reamed him out. Or what he might say. He wasn't planning on changing his mind. This was the best decision for everyone.

A knock on his door startled him out of his stupor. He didn't even know how long he'd been staring at his dark phone he'd yet to turn on.

"Open up, Rider! Now!"

Jason.

Again.

There was no time like the present to get this over with. He'd tell Jason first, then call his captain.

His phone bounced a few times after he tossed it on the cushions, then he strolled to the door as if he didn't have a care in the world. Though he knew if someone had watched him, they would've seen the nerves rushing up and down his spine. His hand even shook as he undid the locks and twisted the knob. Nerves usually didn't attack him. Cool, calm, collected. The job he had, he needed all those traits.

His heart rapped hard against his chest when he saw Junelle standing right next to Jason. His hand reached up without warning and rubbed the usual spot.

"You haven't been answering your phone." Jason looked irate about that fact, then brushed past him as if he'd given him permission to enter.

Jason's jarring movement had caused him to step back, which gave Junelle enough room to walk in without touching him. Thank goodness for that. The tight control he'd kept on his emotions all day long would've crumbled in seconds if she touched him.

She paused in front of him, though didn't say anything. Then she continued on, following Jason and stopping next to him where he'd taken a spot near the couch. Rider caved, closing the door, locking it, and then took position near the kitchen. It gave him a clear view of the front door, but also of his uninvited guests. He never wanted his back to a door again. It also put the couch between them. Jason looked ready for a fight, and Rider wanted to avoid that at all costs.

Jason picked up his phone, pressing on it, then tossed it back down. "You turned your phone off. That answers why you haven't picked up any of my calls. So my next question is why you turned it off?"

"Would you like to sit at the table with me on the other side for this interrogation? It would set the mood more accurately."

Rider knew he was riding a thin line with Jason. Didn't he just tell himself he wanted to avoid a fight? The way Jason squinted foretold he was on his way to fury town. Nothing good ever happened when Jason got that look on his face. It didn't mean it would stop his mouth from running the way it was. He would do anything to get them out of his apartment. That included physically throwing him out, if need be.

"Junelle told me what happened at the precinct."

Rider didn't even bother looking at her. He knew what he'd see. Pity. Disgust. The knowledge that she had been wrong. He wasn't the best detective out there.

"Why didn't you tell us you'd nearly been..."

Killed?

He hated thinking the word as much as Jason couldn't even say it.

"You're hurting and you're doing it alone. Your dad even

said you haven't gone by to see him since you got out of the hospital."

That had his own expression slicing into malice. "You went to see my dad."

Because that was none of Jason's damn business. He'd kept his distance from his dad for a reason. That reason didn't need to be voiced.

"Five years ago that wouldn't have been a big deal. We caught up on a lot. I gave him a piece of my mind too for not telling me you'd been hurt."

"Leave my dad alone!"

He didn't need to drag his father into his mess of a life. When his dad had visited him in the hospital, he couldn't look him in the eye. Because all he'd see was how much he had failed compared to him.

"That man, who could scold both of us with one intense look, didn't even fight back. He is hurting so much that you're even pushing him away. Why, Rider? Why would you push your dad away? Out of everyone?"

"Get out!"

He didn't have to listen to this.

None of it.

"He misses you!"

"Get out!"

"I miss you!"

"Get out!"

"Junelle—"

At the sound of her name, something inside him snapped. The couch didn't stop him. He rushed Jason, taking a swing. Junelle screamed. Jason grunted from the punch. Then he gave as good as he got. They fought each other like they had never been best friends. Maybe it was the lack of food. He hadn't eaten since the granola bar he'd grabbed for breakfast before heading to work. Or maybe because he didn't have as much fight in him as he thought he did. But Jason got the upper hand, pinning him to the floor.

Their heaving breaths was the solitary sound that filled the room for a few minutes. Without warning, Jason got off him, stood up, and held out his hand. He didn't bother grabbing it, but stood up himself. He didn't want Jason's support. Or his friendship. Or his help.

"Leave. I'm removing myself from your sister's case. This will be the last time you see me." He kept his head down as he spoke. He didn't need to see how his news would be taken. Jason would keep fighting him, and he didn't have the energy for that anymore. He had no energy for anything.

Warm hands cupped his cheeks. He sucked in a sharp breath at Junelle's soft touch and closed his eyes. She didn't say a word as she smoothed her hands up and through his hair, eliciting a low groan from him. Then her body moved closer as her hands trailed down his back and stopped. She embraced him, pressing as close as she could to him. Heaven help him, he couldn't stop his own arms from enveloping her in return. They stood there for the longest time. So many things flashed in his mind.

Memories from times best forgotten.

Images of her smiles. Replays of her laughter. The way her body moved beneath his.

A few stray tears might've escaped, but he didn't move his hands from their position to swipe them away.

He didn't know how long they stood there before she let her hands fall and stepped away. Her immediate departure left him bereft. He wanted her back in his arms. Hell, he needed her there.

He still hadn't lifted his head. Not until she put one hand near his heart. The same place he always rubbed.

"I respect your decision. It doesn't mean I like it. You would never let anyone hurt me. Even if you do hate me."

"I don't hate you, June Bug," he whispered, aching to put his hand where her hand rested. He had the intense need to rub the pain away.

Maybe she sensed his mood, because she put pressure on his chest, though didn't rub it.

He couldn't think straight with her standing so close, touching him. He never could. She did something to his senses that made him lose focus.

The sharp, painful inhale that tore from her lips when he backed away hit him square in the gut. It hurt worse than when Jason had pelted him a good one. He'd be sporting some bruises tomorrow.

"I don't respect your decision," Jason growled.

Junelle took a step back and slapped him on the back of the head. "Stop it. You don't know what he's going through. No one does."

They didn't before, but they were getting a clearer picture. He had made sure of that with his many recent outbursts.

"I want my best friend back," Jason muttered like a little boy who's favorite toy had been taken away for being naughty.

Rider shrugged. "I don't know how to be that guy anymore. I...I was distracted that night. I should've had my full focus on Bri. That bastard...he brutally murdered her sister and two other people. I knew what he was capable of. I should've been more focused."

"You can't blame yourself," Junelle said softly, as if that

would lessen the blow of her words. It did nothing to stop the way they hit him in the chest.

"When you walked away, it took a damn long time to move on. A lot longer than I care to admit," he confessed. While he didn't like seeing the agony cross over her features, perhaps it was time to get some things off his chest. "It didn't help that Jason would try reaching out. At times, it made it worse on me. Because, not only did I lose you, I lost my best friend."

"You didn't have to lose me," Jason said, barely holding in the volume of his words.

"Yeah, I did. I would've never been able to see you without Junelle popping up into the equation. I had to move on without either of you." His hand reached up, rubbing his chest. "Then you texted about your parents' anniversary party. Man, I so wanted to respond. I wanted to be there. I stared at that text for the longest time. All day long. Into the evening. On a couch that wasn't mine. At a time when my mind should've been somewhere else."

He saw it in their eyes when they made the connection. Jason had texted him the same day Bri had been attacked and he'd almost been killed. So it wasn't just himself he could blame the situation on. He could blame Jason too.

Not that he did.

He had no one to blame but himself for not being at the top of his game.

"I lose my focus when it comes to you, June Bug. I always have. Right now, I can't afford to do that. I could never..." He swallowed hard, closing his eyes, trying to block out images of her being injured. Or worse, murdered. When he reopened them he had to push away the tears he felt rising to the surface. "I could never see you hurt. It would kill me. I'm not changing my mind."

Junelle nodded. "And I already said I respect that. I won't bother you again. But please, Rider, please try and forgive yourself. No matter what you think, you did nothing wrong."

She walked past Jason, brushing his hand as if wanting to grab it to force him to follow yet putting the decision in his hands.

"And I already said I don't respect it. Now I know it's partly my fault you got hurt. You're not getting rid of me. When we were ten and decided we'd be best friends for life, we swore to each other that nothing would tear us apart. Nothing. We might've been dumbass kids back then, but I'm holding your ass to that promise. Expect to see me tomorrow. And the day after. And the day after. And the day after, until we're both six feet under. And if you still haven't gotten your head out of your ass, I'll haunt you every day until you do. I promise you that."

Then they were gone, and he was alone.

The silence was worse than the noise ever had been.

Despite what he told them, he couldn't wait to see Jason tomorrow.

He needed his best friend back in his life. But he didn't know how to accept it with open arms.

7

"Morning, sunshine."

Junelle glared at her brother as she shuffled into the kitchen. She went straight for the coffee pot, which she knew would be warm and ready for her, even though she hadn't woken up until ten. Her brother took good care of her.

Jason sat at her kitchen table with his laptop open. A few papers were littered around the table as well. She was curious what he was working on, but not enough to ask. Running his own construction company kept him busy. She imagined it had to do with that.

She needed caffeine and then she'd deal with her brother.

After they left Rider's place last night, the ride home had been filled with tension. She wanted to leave Rider alone. He was struggling, but she didn't know how to help the person she witnessed yesterday. She didn't know that man. Honestly, she was the last person he wanted help from.

Jason, on the other hand, wanted to get into his face until he caved, as if that brutal way would work.

They didn't speak much either when they got home. She retreated to her room and didn't come out until now.

She took a few sips of coffee before taking a seat at the table. Jason's intense stare made her want to wiggle in her seat, but she forced herself to remain still.

"Your eyes are red."

Well, he wasn't a detective, but he had good observation skills. That's what she wanted to say. Instead, she took another sip of coffee.

Of course, her eyes were bloodshot. She cried last night. A lot. Like she did the night before. But this time it hadn't been about Molly. Rider held her attention all evening long.

The tears spilled from the lost years she didn't have to lose. All because of her reaction to something that could've been resolved by speaking to him. Having an adult conversation.

Then more tears released from the thought he could've died and she would've never had a chance to make amends. Though he said he forgave her and didn't hate her, she still didn't feel like things were right between them. Or maybe that was her deep wishful thinking they could try one more time at a relationship. That's why things didn't feel right. He wasn't back in her life and in her arms where he belonged.

The last round of tears had been for the torment he lived in. At the mental anguish he put himself through every day for something he had no control over.

While her eyes told the epic story of her crying episode, she wasn't about to talk about any of that with her brother.

"I tried calling Rider this morning. He didn't answer."

"He's not going to, Jason. Leave him be."

Jason slammed the lid to his computer down. "What is wrong with you?"

Her brows drew together, trying to decipher such an odd

question. Where would he like her to start? Because so many things in her life were currently wrong.

"Aren't you going to fight for him?"

"Fight for him?"

Jason leaned back, crossing his arms. "I mean, you never stopped loving him, so yeah, Junelle, fight for him."

She'd never confessed she loved Rider. Not to anyone. Not even Rider himself.

"I'm not an idiot. I had an inkling about you two back then. Now that it's all in the open..." Jason sat up straight, bending toward her. "I see it in your eyes. You love him. You always did. Sure, you messed up. But you apologized and he forgives you. Now you—"

"I need to leave him alone," she cut him off, not wanting to hear anything else. "That's what he wants. He might've forgiven me, but it doesn't mean he wants me back in his life."

A strangled laugh echoed between them. Jason shook his head as if he couldn't believe what she was saying. "The second you touched him, I saw him relax. The tension in his body evaporated. You had to have felt it."

Yeah, maybe she did.

But it didn't mean anything.

"It's always been like that with you two. When you were in a tizzy, Rider calmed you down. When his emotions were ramped up, you settled him down. He might be saying 'leave me the hell alone' but it's not what he wants. Trust me."

And if she put her trust in her brother's words and it was the furthest thing from the truth, she'd never recover from it. It took her forever to move on from him when she thought the worst of him. Even then, her heart had never truly let him go. Letting him in again, only to lose him— how would she survive the devastation a second time?

"Can we please talk about something else?"

The doorbell ringing answered her question. At least for the moment.

"Saved by the doorbell," Jason muttered with frustration as he stood up from the table. "We'll be circling back to the conversation later."

"Yippy." She rolled her eyes and swirled her pointer finger around in a circle.

Jason glared at her sarcasm, and she knew it wouldn't deter him from picking up the chat later.

When she heard Detective Stromberg's voice, she jumped up from the table and made her way to the foyer. Deflation hit her system, but she tried to hide it by lifting her coffee mug to her lips before greeting Detective Stromberg and Powell. Rider had kept his word. He wasn't working her case any longer. Otherwise, he would've been in attendance as well.

"Good morning, Junelle," Detective Stromberg said with a short smile, though it didn't reach his eyes.

By the somber expression they both wore, she knew something else had happened.

"We should sit," Stromberg said, gesturing toward the living room.

She didn't have it in her to argue. Apparently, neither did Jason. They all took a seat, and she didn't shove off Jason's arm when he wrapped it around her as if he also sensed they were about to impart some terrible news.

"Do you know Paul Champston?" Stromberg asked.

Junelle nodded. "He works at the theater doing costumes." Her back straightened as it hit her. "He's the one who killed Molly?"

She couldn't picture it. Paul was the nicest guy in the world. He brought in homemade treats on occasion for no reason at all. Other times he did because he knew someone was celebrating a birthday. He opened doors for everyone. Even if someone looked not the most appealing in an outfit, he had a way of making them feel beautiful nonetheless. He would never send those vulgar letters and kill her dog. Never!

Stromberg cleared his throat and shook his head. "He was found murdered this morning."

The coffee mug slipped from her fingers, dropping to the floor. She felt the coffee hit her pajama pants, soaking them, but the mess below didn't penetrate. His dreadful words echoed in her mind, blocking everything else out.

"According to the detectives handling the case—it's a different precinct from us—it appears to have been a robbery. Multiple things were missing from his home."

Jason's arm had tightened around her, hugging her closer. "So not related with Junelle?"

"We can't rule that out," Detective Powell replied. "It appears to look like a robbery. But, if I'm being honest, I don't buy it."

The two detectives shared a look as if silently having a word with each other. As if Stromberg didn't want Powell to be saying such things.

"Why do you think that?" She hated how timid she sounded.

The detectives shared another look before Powell responded. "He was tied up. Whoever broke in didn't need to hurt him. But they did. Violently."

Like they had done to Molly. She could see it in his eyes, that's what he wanted to add.

"I also don't like coincidences," Detective Powell continued. "I find it hard to believe it's not all related."

Jason didn't let up his hold on her, but he shifted in his

seat, his body tensing. "Why would this person kill Paul? It makes no sense."

"That's why we're here," Stromberg said, adding a smile as if that would help the situation, "to find out why. How close were you with Paul?"

She shrugged. "We were friendly. Chatted and whatnot. We didn't hang outside of work or anything. We both work on different projects now and again. We're not always on the same production. He was a wonderful guy. He would've done anything for anyone. I don't understand why anyone would hurt him."

"Did he ever ask you out?" Powell asked.

"No. Never. He was dating...ummm...Emily something for a while. He seemed happy. But they broke up a few months ago. I didn't ask why and he didn't offer the details."

"No trouble with him? Any complaints?" Powell continued.

"No, again, he was a great guy. I can't imagine anyone has anything bad to say about him."

"This makes no sense," Jason muttered, blowing out a heavy breath. "Where's Rider?"

At that idiotic question, Junelle tensed and wanted to shove her brother away. She didn't, though, not wanting to raise more questions for the detectives. Not that it would take a genius to figure out why she was irritated.

"Taking the day off," Tate replied smoothly, as if Rider had never stepped back from the case and had no intention of doing so. Then he stood up. "If we have more questions, we'll be back. We're not the ones working Paul's case, but we will be keeping a close eye on it. I suggest you take a few more days off of work for the time being."

They walked them to the door, but she didn't register anything else they said. Then they were gone.

"I need to clean the carpet."

She turned, but Jason stopped her before she could get very far.

"I won't let anyone hurt you. I don't know what the hell is going on, but you're safe, Junelle."

She jerked her head she understood but said nothing else. What was there to say? She knew her brother would do everything in his power to keep her safe. She never doubted that.

But why was someone doing this?

Why would someone kill Paul? How could it possibly relate to her?

None of it made sense, and trying to decipher it caused a headache, so she tried to block it all out.

That made her mind swirl to Rider.

That wasn't any better to focus on either.

The tears came right in the middle of her scrubbing as hard as she could into the carpet to get the dark stain out. Uncontrollable sobs that wracked her body. Not even Jason's warm arms around her abated them.

HE BLEW out a breath before hitting the voicemail button.

"What the hell, man? Why weren't you here today? We need you. Junelle needs you. Do you even know one of her co-worker's was killed today? Do you even care? Answer your damn phone!"

Rider hit the delete button and then tossed his phone to the side.

He should've deleted Jason's damn message before listening to it, but he didn't. Nor the other twenty or so messages he'd left. Talk about torturing himself.

Stromberg had called twice and left three text messages. Tate sent one text message. Short and sweet. "You're welcome."

That one he had a hard time figuring out. What did he even mean by that? After realizing there were no messages from his captain from this morning or even yesterday, he assumed Tate had given the captain some excuse about his absence that didn't give him cause to worry. Well, whatever. He wasn't going to give his thanks. Because in the end, it was delaying the inevitable.

Turning in his badge.

If he couldn't work this one case, fear of screwing up so horrible, how could he work any of his other cases? Simple. He couldn't. Therefore, he had to quit. He had to hand in his gun and badge and walk away before he messed up again.

When he found the courage, anyway. That wasn't something he had found yet. He loved his job so damn much.

He'd left his phone off all night long. Not that it helped him any. He couldn't sleep. He couldn't eat. He didn't do anything but stare at the ceiling for the longest time and pace his bedroom before he went back to lying down and staring at the ceiling once more. Back and forth he went between both actions. After drinking a full pot of coffee, he was wired, yet dead tired. Maybe it was more anxious energy coursing through his veins rather than wired energy. Whatever it was, it kept his eyes open, staring into space.

And into his phone since turning it back on this morning.

Because the one person he wanted to reach out hadn't— Junelle. Which was for the best. Even if she had called or left a text message, he wouldn't have answered. What was there to say?

A knock on his door had him turning his attention in

that direction, but he didn't move a muscle from his spot on the couch.

"We're not going away until you open the door, asshole," Tate muttered from the other side.

Knowing Tate, he'd break down his door to say his piece in his face. That knowledge gave him the energy to get up and open the door for his colleagues he wished would leave him alone.

"You look like shit," Tate commented with a cheery smile as he walked past him.

Stromberg grimaced and then tried to smile as if that would erase Tate's rudeness. He didn't care. Tate could say whatever he wanted, however he wanted, and it wasn't going to snap him out of the hole he'd fallen into.

"You hear what happened?" Tate asked, taking the lead on this intervention—meeting, visit, whatever they wanted to call it.

Rider decided playing dumb wouldn't get him anywhere other than making their stay longer. "I did."

Paul Champston, a co-worker of Junelle's, had been murdered late last night. The detectives on the case thought it was a robbery gone bad. Not that he believed that for one minute. Nor would he explain what he knew or how he knew it. Because despite trying to focus on anything other than Junelle and her case last night, all he did was immerse himself in it.

"Get dressed so we can get this bastard already." Tate tossed his head toward the hallway as if Rider needed directions on how to find his bedroom.

He was dressed in sweats and a black T-shirt. No socks. The clothing on his body would stay right where it was. Like he'd stay right where he was.

By Tate's comment, they didn't believe it wasn't related

either. They were looking for the same culprit that murdered Molly.

"Please, Rider." Stromberg's voice was calmer and quieter, but no less effective. He didn't move a muscle.

"I haven't called the captain yet—"

"No need to," Tate cut him off. "I told him you had a twenty-four-hour bug and would be back at it soon. You're welcome."

Well, his instincts had been right. Tate's one-worded message was for covering his ass at work. Still wasn't getting a thanks from him. And to avoid getting cut off again, he'd keep his words short and sweet from now on.

"I'm quitting."

Stromberg's eyes widened in surprise. Tate looked a bit surprised himself, his jaw even dropping a fraction.

"If I can't effectively do my job, I shouldn't be on the job."

"I'm sorry, man," Stromberg said, the sorrow spilling out, telling him he wasn't faking his emotions. Not that he thought Stromberg would fake such a thing. "I had no idea how much we all failed you. You've been drowning in pain, and we've let you. I'm done doing that. You're not quitting."

A merciful laugh escaped before he could stop it. "And how are you going to stop me?"

Stromberg had no retort to that. Tate looked ready to pummel a few fists into his face, he was clenching his jaw so hard.

Then Tate spoke.

"You remember the first time you met me? Abby?"

Oh, he remembered. A man, Brandan something—he couldn't remember his full name—had been shot outside a pub. He'd suspected Abby, Tate's girlfriend, having something to do with it since she had been standing by the man when he'd been shot. Considering a sniper had shot him, he knew Abby hadn't shot the guy herself. But she had been a part of it somehow. He could never figure out how, but the gnawing in his gut had never disappeared. The case remained unsolved to this day. Tate hadn't been a detective with the NYPD then, but he'd acted like he owned the damn city. Rider hadn't liked the guy from the first moment he met him.

He nodded, not sure where Tate was going with this line of questioning.

"Abby said she didn't know the guy who got shot."

"Witnesses said otherwise." Which was why Rider always suspected something fishy had been going on there that day.

"They were right."

Rider's eyes narrowed. "What's the point here? Other than you two lied straight to my face and every other cop there that day." Damn, he also felt such immense satisfaction that he'd been right.

"My point is that you're not the only one who feels guilt. Who regrets their actions. That lives daily with the knowledge they should've done something else instead of what they actually did. Our actions always have consequences. There's no getting around that."

"So Abby knew the guy? And she feels guilty for knowing him?" Rider had no idea what the hell he was talking about.

Tate stepped closer, lowering his voice and softening his features as if they had a large audience and he didn't want anyone else to hear anything. "This doesn't leave the room. Understand?"

He jerked his head once. He sensed it was something he had to agree to if he wanted Tate to get to the point.

"She was searching for her brother, Cooper. She knew he had killed all those women. That her brother was a serial killer. So she went to an old friend who could've helped her find him. And Cooper wasn't a man known for letting things slide. He needed to send his sister a message. To leave him the hell alone. So he killed that man without blinking, knowing his sister would understand clearly what he wanted. For her to back off. That the next bullet would be for her."

It all clicked together. The friend had been Brandan—the man murdered outside the pub. A cold case that he thought would've continued to get colder and colder.

And now he knew the truth. Cooper killed him. One more person in a long line of victims.

Which was why Tate told him nothing could leave this room. Odd though. Even though Cooper was dead, who cared if it came out he'd killed Brandan? They'd pinned so many other murders on him. It wouldn't be a big deal.

Rider knew the big deal was Abby and how she had lied to the police. He'd keep his secret. It wasn't hurting anyone, so it didn't matter.

"How much guilt do you think she carries around? A shit ton! Do you think she doesn't have nightmares at times because of it? Because she damn well does! Do you think she doesn't regret that she never went to him? Every damn day! But she doesn't let that guilt bring her down. She doesn't let it consume her." Tate stood less than a foot away now. He'd been inching closer as he spoke, so engaged in every word he said that Rider hadn't even been aware.

"You shouldn't let it consume you either. Shit happened. You got hurt, and I know it kills you. But you can't let it eat you alive. You can't." Tate ran a hand down his face, swearing under his breath. "Excuse me."

Then he stalked out of his apartment, slamming the door on his way out.

Stromberg watched his partner exit, staring at the door for a few seconds before turning his attention his way. "He's calling Abby. Before Briella, I would've never understood how anyone could love someone so much. To the point that it can physically hurt you."

Oh, he understood that pain well. Thinking Junelle's name sent a wave of fresh pain straight to his heart.

"Those two are pretty good liars."

His comment made Stromberg laugh. It was true though. They'd lied straight to his face about the entire case. Stromberg's too.

"How long have you known the truth on that case?"

Stromberg rubbed his chin, wincing. "A long time."

Ridiculous. "I'm sensing there's more I don't know about Tate, isn't there?"

"He might come off as a hardass and someone who doesn't care, but it's a facade. He cares deeply about too much. Especially Abby. There's nothing he wouldn't do for her."

"That wasn't a direct yes or no, but I'm taking it as a yes."

Stromberg chuckled, while the laughter in his eyes said he wouldn't be giving a concrete answer. "I don't know the history between you and Junelle, but I sense you'd do anything for her. The fact you knew about Paul this morning before we got here confirms it. Are you prepared to walk away? Because that's not the Rider I know. I know you're hurting. Because you're not letting anyone help. Let us help you."

When he said nothing in return, Stromberg left as well.

What an interesting turn of events. He'd solved a cold case without meaning to. Not that he could mark it solved.

That would raise questions he didn't want to answer. But in his mind, he'd solved it and could move it to the done pile.

And they gave him a lot more to think about. Damn them!

Of course he couldn't walk away from Junelle. Problem was he didn't know how to walk toward her either.

8

"GET YOUR SHOES ON."

Junelle was curled up on her bed underneath the comforter. She'd come upstairs after supper to read, or at least, that's what she told her brother. The book still rested on her nightstand. She needed time to herself. The night had been a remorseful one after learning of Paul's death. While she wanted to comfort her co-workers in person, she wasn't ready to leave the house. Nor did Jason want her to leave either. So she settled for calling and texting people, offering condolences and asking questions.

No one knew anything more than she did, and she had spoken to the detectives. Though not the ones handling the case. They had been by the theater to question people, but they hadn't been by her house. Maybe because Stromberg and Powell had. She didn't know, and it took too much effort to wonder why.

Between crying and cleaning her house like a maniac that didn't *need* to be cleaned, she'd exhausted herself. After supper, something she couldn't even remember what Jason had made and that she barely touched, she needed to get away. Have time to herself.

To cry again in the comfort of her solitude.

Now her brother wanted her to put her shoes on. No. She wasn't leaving.

"Now, Junelle," he said as he yanked the covers back.

She grabbed for them, trying to put them where they'd been, but he refused to allow her to.

"I can't leave you alone and I need to go."

She sat up, her eyes narrowing. "Where?"

"You know where. Now get your shoes on." He walked out of her room, his voice trailing as he added, "And change your clothes if you want. Doesn't matter to me, but we're going. Pajamas or no pajamas."

She looked down at her plain white T-shirt and then trailed down to her pink pants with dancing llamas sprinkled all over it. *Ugh!* She wanted to despise her brother right now for forcing her to leave. Because, yeah, she knew where he wanted to go.

Rider's!

The last place they should be going. Rider asked for them to leave him alone, and she wanted to respect that. The last thing she needed was to push him further away. Perhaps when things died down and all the craziness was over, she could try again to be friends. But pushing a man when he was already sitting on the edge of a cliff didn't seem wise.

But her brother wasn't giving her an option.

She wouldn't be thanking him for the reminder to change! The hell she would!

After staring at her closet for far longer than she meant to, she settled on her favorite pair of jeans—the ones that made her ass look good—and a green shirt that fit her every curve and brought out the color of her eyes. She even stopped in the bathroom to apply a touch of makeup. One, she had to cover the redness from all the crying somehow. Two, she wanted to look semi-decent if she was going to see Rider again.

Twenty-five minutes later, she strolled downstairs and to the front door where Jason stood with a sappy grin.

He looked at his watch, then at her. "For someone who looked ready to fight to the death to have to leave the house, you sure dolled yourself up. And took your time doing it."

"Shut up."

She followed his laughter as they left the house. When they settled in his car, he paused before driving off.

"You look beautiful."

"I look like I've been crying all day."

Jason laid a hand on her shoulder. "For good reason. It doesn't take the beauty away."

She met his gaze. "We shouldn't bother him. He needs space."

"What he needs is to get his head out of his ass. Remember when his mom died?"

How could she forget? It had been a horrible moment in his life. She'd never seen such a strong, capable man cry like he did the day he left the hospital. He cried in her arms until he must've realized what he was doing and she'd never seen another tear emerge. He drew away from people, from life. He wouldn't leave the house for a week before Jason came tearing in, making him. His dad had been no help because he'd been in the same insurmount-able pain.

"Of course I remember."

"Then you know he didn't go through any of that alone. If we would've let him, he'd still be holed up in his room in the back of his dad's house. He needs us. Not some damn space!"

With those fiery words, her brother pulled away from the curb.

She knew he was right. But it felt odd trying to help a man who hadn't been in her life for the longest time. For a man who didn't seem to want her back in his life.

It terrified her. For the moment when he would demand she leave and to never come back. Turn the tables and do the same thing she had done to him.

By the time they made it to his apartment, her nerves were bouncing like a live wire cut from a line and she wanted to puke. Jason's determined strides renewed part of her bravery. But after he banged on the door and Rider opened it, all that recharged bravery fled. He didn't even look in her direction.

She wanted to laugh at the way he rolled his eyes and walked away from the door, knowing Jason wouldn't leave without gaining entry first.

"Any news on the case?" Jason asked, waltzing into the kitchen like he had a right to. Like they hadn't been apart for five years as best friends.

Rider cocked a brow at his audacity when Jason opened the fridge and grabbed some beers. She stood to the side, waiting to see how this all played out. Jason didn't give her a beer, knowing she didn't like it, but he handed one to Rider, then opened his own.

"Well?" Jason asked after taking a long swallow.

Rider looked at him, then the beer in his hand as if he couldn't remember how it got there in the first place. Then his gaze darted back to Jason. "No."

Jason laughed. "That's all I get is a no?" Jason's gaze trailed up and down Rider. Based on the fact he was wearing sweats and a T-shirt, wondering if he even left the apartment to work on the case. "What did you do all day?"

"Can we not do this?" Rider lifted his hand, rubbing his chest. She wanted to place her hand there instead to stop him from the movement. She hated witnessing his pain like that. Except she didn't move a muscle.

"Did you or did you not work on my sister's case today?"

Well, she would say he didn't, considering he said yesterday he was not going to. But again, she stayed silent as she knew it'd be a losing battle with her brother. When he got something in his head, there was no stopping him.

Rider also knew how her brother operated because he remained silent. No amount of arguing would sway him. His silence also was the answer. No, he hadn't worked on her case today.

Jason slammed the rest of the bottle in one large swallow, then set it on the dining room table. "I have to run a few errands. Watch Junelle for me. Thanks."

Then he walked out before either of them could protest.

What the hell just happened?

She stared at the door wondering if her brother had lost his damn mind. First he interrogated Rider, and then he dropped the conversation and left her alone with him.

The nerves she thought were pulsating before with earnest jumped to a full-blown vengeance as she turned her head toward Rider. He looked as confused as her. But for the first time that night, he was looking directly at her.

"I had no idea he was going to leave me here. If I would've known, I would've asked my friends to come over. I know you don't want me here. I respect that. I do. You know how Jason gets—"

"It's okay," Rider interrupted, his voice low and soothing

as if he knew one loud, abrupt word would send her off the deep end. "I have wine if you want a glass."

He knew her as well as her own brother. She inclined her head in acceptance instead of using her voice. Another word and she knew she'd keep rambling until he was forced to cut her off again.

She sat on the couch while he went to the kitchen. The soft sounds he made sent her back in time to the moments they'd shared quiet evenings.

Then she was thrust out of the memories when he sat down next to her, holding out a glass of white wine.

"Thank you."

He'd twisted the cap off his beer, then gestured a welcome in return. They sat in silence for the longest time.

"I still haven't located the owner of the car."

She twisted so she didn't have to strain her neck.

"I heard about your co-worker as well. I'm sorry. Were you close?"

"We were friends. Not outside of work or anything, but we were friends. He was a good guy."

Rider fiddled with the bottle. "I didn't go to work today."

But he still worked if his first comment about not finding the owner of the car was any indication.

"I'm trying hard to back away from this case. From everything."

Oh, how she wanted to pull him into her arms and erase all the agony she could hear.

Then his gaze connected with hers. "No matter how hard I tried, I couldn't do it. The thought of you getting hurt...I—"

She reached up and cupped his cheek. His eyes closed as he leaned into it. "I understand if you have to walk away. It's okay."

His eyes snapped open. "It's not. When it comes to you, it's not okay. I—"

"It's okay that—"

"No, June Bug, don't cut me off again. Let me finish. I want to keep you safe, but I'm afraid I can't. I couldn't even keep Bri safe. I let her down. I hate myself for that. I've already let you down once. To do it again...I'm terrified."

There was no coffee table to set her wineglass down, so she set it on the floor, then moved so close to him, she was in his lap. Her hands grasped his cheeks so he couldn't look away because he might want to try.

"The only one who let someone down between us was me. I failed *you*. By not trusting you. And if we're talking about hate, then I hate myself for breaking the trust I should've had for you."

HOW MANY TIMES had he told her already they should leave the past in the past and move on? One sentence from him and it was bringing it back to the forefront. It wasn't the conversation he wanted to have. Hell, he didn't even want to talk about the current case.

All he wanted to do was set his beer down, pull her farther into his arms, and kiss her breathless.

Since he couldn't do that, he gripped his bottle tighter.

"Rider..."

Oh, God. Why did she have to whisper his name with such longing? The same intense ache he felt in his gut.

"I don't think Paul's death is unrelated."

Junelle blinked rapidly, as if surprised by the abrupt change, then dropped her hands and sat back out of reach.

"Detective Stromberg and Powell mentioned the same thing."

Crisis averted. At least, the sexual one. He wasn't sure venturing forth down this path was any better.

"You were targeted with nasty letters. Then your dog is killed. Now someone you work with was murdered. Too many damn coincidences. I don't believe in coincidences."

"Why would someone kill Paul because of me?"

Rider shrugged. He'd been wondering the same thing all day long. "You said he was a good guy. You never had any problems with him? Did he ask you out?"

"No. Never. I already told Detective Stromberg and Powell these things."

He looked down at his beer bottle. While not intoned with derision or irritation, he felt the blow from her answer, nonetheless. He should know all the answers because he should've been with those two from the beginning.

"I'm sorry. I didn't mean anything by that."

"I'm not on the case anymore anyway. It's no big deal."

He flinched when she touched his leg, but he didn't look up at her.

"I've never had any problems with Paul. We've worked on some of the same productions throughout our career and he's always been wonderful to work with. He's never asked me out and I've never gotten the feeling he wanted to. He dated a woman by the name of Emily for the longest time, but I believe they broke up a few months ago. I have nothing bad to say about him. I'm baffled why someone would hurt him, especially if it has something to do with me."

All that information further confused him as well. He agreed. It didn't make sense to lash out at Paul when he had no issues with Junelle.

He felt pressure on his leg where her hand rested, but he

still couldn't find the strength to move his gaze from the beer bottle.

"I wish I could help you somehow. I hate seeing you like this. So down on yourself. I don't know Detective Stromberg and Powell, and I want to trust them working my case. I do in a sense. While you're right, I don't know how good of a detective you are, I know *you*. At least, I did. The man I knew I trusted with my whole heart." She paused. No doubt because of what she said. Because she hadn't trusted him. One incident and she threw that trust away.

"I was wrong five years ago. I should've trusted you. I should've given you a chance to explain. And a long time might've passed, but I know you're that same man. I know it. Please don't stop working my case. I feel safer knowing you're working on it."

Oh, how he wanted to believe those words. He wanted to absorb them straight to his soul, erasing the darkness that had taken a hold of him.

That ache that always hit his chest, pulsated right on cue. Before his brain could inform his hand to reach up and rub, it's as if Junelle sensed what he wanted to do. Her hand lifted from his leg and touched his chest. Instead of rubbing like he did, she held her palm still but with pressure.

"I don't deserve it. A second chance. But I'm here for you. Tell me what to do and—"

"Oh, June Bug..." he whispered before losing the fight with his control. He dropped the beer bottle to the floor, not even taking care to set it down. Then he grabbed her around the waist and pulled her into his arms. Though he longed for a kiss, he settled with a crushing hug, tucking his face into the crook of her neck.

She trembled and sank into his embrace.

For the first time in the longest time—five years to be

exact—his world felt like it went back onto the correct axis. Everything would be okay as long as she was in his arms. That's what his heart told him. But his brain argued things weren't that simple.

"No second chances."

She stiffened at his muffled words.

He had no idea why they came out of his mouth. It didn't mean what she thought it meant. From the moment they spoke of the past, he'd wanted to forget everything that happened. In doing so, it meant they could pick up right where they left off, which meant no second chances were required. Except his brain didn't formulate that all correctly to his mouth and it came out all wrong.

Which was for the best. If he was going to protect Junelle, he needed his head in the game. Everything—especially his overwrought emotions—needed to stay in check. He couldn't afford to lose focus.

She was back in his life, and when this was all over, he'd make sure it stayed that way. He'd never stopped loving her. Not for one moment, even if she had crushed his heart.

He leaned back so he could look at her, but he didn't let go. Deciding to ignore those idiotic words, he'd tell her something that would make her forget everything else.

"I'll stay on the case."

She relaxed in his arms, but the hurt lingered.

So okay, she didn't forget what he said, but it was best not to move forward with that line of talk. If he remained on the case, he needed all his wits about him. He wouldn't be able to do that if she was in his arms.

Shit!

Which she currently was.

He let his arms drop and then put her back on her side

of the couch. More pain filtered into her expression. He ignored it as he stood up.

"I made a mess."

Of course, he meant the bottle he'd dropped, soaking beer into his carpet. But the things between him and Junelle were also insinuated in that comment.

The room remained silent while he cleaned up the liquid that had saturated into his beige carpet. No stain remained, so at least there was that. Not that he would've cared either way.

When he sat back down—albeit no beer this time—he didn't know what to say. How to proceed. He picked up her wine glass, hoping the extra barrier would keep them apart, and handed it to her. She took it without a word of thanks. She even took a sip.

More silence filled the area.

He wished he knew what to say.

Junelle drank more of her wine, depleting half the glass. Then she sighed, resigned to the box he'd put them in. Friends only. If they were lucky to even venture into friendship. It would be best to stay away from that as well. Safer for all involved.

"Thank you, Rider. I already feel better knowing you're staying on the case."

Yeah, well, he didn't have all his confidence back yet, but he wasn't going to admit that. Not to her, anyway. He needed her to believe everything would be okay. Because seeing any kind of fear in her gutted him straight to the core.

Stromberg's parting words filtered through his mind. He'd been right, even if Rider hadn't confirmed it.

"I'd do anything for you, June Bug. Absolutely anything."

9

RIDER DIDN'T SAY a word as he walked to his desk and took a seat. Stromberg and Tate stared at him the entire time, but they remained silent as well. They didn't ask why he came into work this morning. They didn't ask what had changed his mind. They didn't comment on how he looked dead-ass tired—though his mind was intact and ready to tackle the day.

Jason had returned shortly after he and Junelle had their emotional talk. Neither said what transpired between, but he knew Junelle would tell her brother everything on the way home. Well, maybe not the part where he'd insinuated they would never get back together. She'd keep that to herself.

He hated having that wedge between them, but for the time being it was for the best. It would keep her safe.

After signing into the system, finding the information he'd gotten last night, and printing it off, he headed to Stromberg and Tate's desk. Then he set the piece of paper down for them to see.

"Roger Woodson. Owner of the vehicle from the video.

Also happens to work security at the theater where Junelle and Paul works."

Tate cocked a brow as Stromberg picked up the driver's license photo of their prime suspect. It had taken him working all through the night, from the moment Junelle and Jason left, to find the culprit. After sifting through license plate after license plate, he decided to try another avenue.

He woke up Detective Cramer, one of the detectives on Paul's murder, at one in the morning demanding the list of people they'd already interviewed and who worked at the theater. Despite Detective Cramer reaming him out for waking him up—and his five-month-old son—he begrudgingly handed over the information.

From there, it was simply looking up the registration for every person on the list. He got a hit with Roger Woodson, confirming Paul's murder was not a coincidence. Why had he been driving around Junelle's neighborhood? Why did he kill Junelle's dog? Why kill Paul? Why send her those threatening letters? So many questions, and Rider would get to the bottom of each one.

Stromberg handed the photo to Tate, nodding as a low chuckle escaped. "Nice job, man."

Rider's second call to Detective Cramer went even worse than the first call when he informed Cramer that Paul's case was now his. He even hung up the phone as Cramer ranted and raved in his ear. It was connected to Junelle's case, therefore he wasn't even going to argue for a second about it.

"Paul's case is now ours. Let's go pick up Roger."

Tate laughed, the paper floating to his desk as he dropped it. "Does Cramer and Jackson know that?"

"I informed Cramer this morning. So he can relay it to Jackson." Once he got over being pissed about it, he'd let his partner know they were off the case.

Stromberg and Tate stood up. Captain Wilson walked into the area at the same time, barking, "Rider! My office! Now!"

He knew this was coming, but it didn't bother him. The captain could say whatever he wanted, but it wouldn't matter. He wasn't going to stop investigating this case until Junelle was safe. One moment of weakness, damn near walking away, would never happen again. He was committed to seeing this through all the way to the end.

Footsteps followed him, along with short chuckles and low murmurs. Stromberg and Tate were hot on his heels, even though the captain hadn't asked for them.

When they stepped into the captain's office behind him, the captain flicked his hand for them to leave. "I didn't say you two."

"Well, Captain, we're all working together, so whatever you say to him applies to us too," Tate said without breaking a sweat, as if he never feared anything.

"So when I ream his ass for dodging work a full day—knowing quite well he didn't have a twenty-four-hour bug," the captain said, his brow rising with fury at Tate, "then pissing on another detective's case, one not even in our precinct, then all that applies to you too? Is that what you're saying?"

Tate didn't flinch once. "Yep."

Captain Wilson slowly moved his attention to him. "You can't just take over another detective's case. I got Captain Grover up my ass that his detectives are being harassed by you and to back the hell off. So I expect you to do that. All three of you!" He held up his hand when Tate looked ready to speak again. "And I know how hard that is for you three. Following orders. For once in your life, do it. Make my job easier."

Rider glanced at Stromberg and Tate. Neither wore expressions that were easy to decipher. Impassive, like him. Then he looked back at the captain.

"Respectively, Captain, Paul Champston's murder is connected with one of ours. Molly Swanson. It would be beneficial for the police to consolidate these two cases so our efforts can go to more cases needing attention. Considering our case appeared first, it makes the most sense we take point on it."

Captain Wilson's mouth thinned into a tight line, glancing between all three of them. "Respectively," he started, emphasizing that word with sarcasm, "the murder of a dog, *Molly Swanson*, shouldn't even be a case on your desk, Detective Rider."

Okay. So naming Junelle's dog as if it were a person did not get by the captain. But whatever. What he said remained the same. Their case popped up first. They should get first dibs on any other related cases.

"And your fancy words and articulate sentences isn't going to change my mind. Back off the Paul Champston case. Now!"

"And if I don't, Captain?" His hand ached to reach up and rub his chest, but he fought the impulse hard. He had to stop doing that.

"Remember that request to make my job easier?" Captain Wilson sat back, sinking into his chair with a heavy sigh. "I can say one thing and you three are going to walk out of here and still do whatever the hell you want. Aren't you?"

Not one of them answered. Which was answer enough.

"Let me make myself clear. If I hear from Captain Grover again, you're suspended. All three of you. I don't care who

Captain Grover names. If one of you steps out of line, you all get the consequences."

They still didn't respond.

"Get the hell out and go do your jobs!" Captain Wilson threw a hand toward the door. "And by jobs, I mean all of them but the Paul Champston case!"

They walked out single file with Stromberg leading the way. Rider closed the door on his way out. They stopped at the end of the hallway at a crossways. Left to the exit and right to their desks.

"You two can do whatever the hell you want, but I'm going to go pick up Roger Woodson."

Tate nodded. "And how are you going to do that without pissing off Cramer?"

"The way I see it, Woodson's still a suspect in Junelle's stalker case. It is his car in the video that was obtained near her house. Blood was visible on his person, indicating he had something to do with Molly's death. Cramer can't say anything about that."

"Good point," Stromberg said. "And while we're chatting, if Paul's case happens to come up, then it does."

Tate clapped his hands, smirking. "Just like you love having a plan, Stromberg, I love having a plan. I'll drive."

They followed him out of the precinct.

"Glad to see you back at work today," Stromberg said as they made their way to the car.

He'd never admit it out loud, but it was good to be back. Why he ever thought he could up and quit was beyond him. This job was everything to him. He lived and breathed every moment.

Of course that was before Junelle had walked back into his life. He had needed something to devote his attention to.

Something to take his mind off the pain. Now that she had reappeared...

Well, not something he should think about. He needed his entire focus on the case so he could keep her safe.

"What changed your mind?" Stromberg continued, not ready to let the conversation go despite his silence.

Again, he'd never say it was Junelle and *only* Junelle that had changed his mind. He didn't want anyone to know the kind of power she held over him. Especially her. Though she had to know the effect she had on him.

And shit. So did Jason, otherwise he wouldn't have shown up last night with Junelle in tow. He should've known back then Jason knew everything.

He opened the back passenger door, holding back a flinch when Stromberg grabbed the top of the frame to stop him from shutting it.

"You can ignore my questions, it's fine. But I'm damn glad to see you back." Then he let go and opened his own door, sliding into the front passenger seat.

Rider still didn't respond as he took his own seat, but he agreed.

It was damn good to be back.

He'd never walk away from his job again. It was time to stop with his pity party and move on. The pain and guilt from what happened with Bri still lived inside of him. It wouldn't be easily erased. If ever. He had a daily reminder of what happened every time he looked in the mirror and saw the scars on his chest.

But the more he talked about it, the more he heard the comforting words from Junelle, the more the guilt receded.

Yeah, she had all the power to control him. It was best he never let her know that. Because she could destroy him with ease.

There was no way he wanted to live through that kind of devastation again.

***

SHIT. Shit. Shit.

He might've made a mistake. Killing Paul, while enjoyable and much needed, brought undue attention he couldn't afford to have.

Charles meowed, trying to circle his feet as he paced in the kitchen.

He'd ransacked Paul's house before leaving. Stole jewelry and money that he could find. Unhooked the TV, though didn't take it. He wanted to make it seem like he had planned to. He grabbed the computer and tablet he found. Going from room to room, he made sure to make it appear like the place had been searched from top to bottom for valuables. A robbery gone bad. Afterward, he ditched all the stuff in the garbage on the other side of town. He didn't keep one thing from Paul's. He wasn't a thief. Well, in that instance he wasn't. He would—and had—steal when necessary.

Except the police showed up to the theater yesterday. Interviewed everyone!

Why?

They had no reason to come to Paul's work. It was a robbery. Plain and simple. Why couldn't the cops see that?

Meow.

He cursed, tripping when Charles stepped into his path. Inhaling a deep breath, he then let it out before losing control. It wasn't Charles' fault he was upset.

"Let me feed you. Papa's sorry." He gave Charles a few

rubs on the back before grabbing the cat food and filling his bowl. Fresh water as well.

Charles didn't hesitate, gobbling up the food with haste.

With that done, he resumed his pacing. The microwave clock told him he had ten minutes before he should leave for work.

But what would happen if the cops showed up again? He'd kept his cool yesterday, answering questions and appearing as calm and normal as he could. Would that same demeanor remain today? He wasn't so sure. The anger was building up again. Like a geyser on the precipice of blowing.

This was Paul's fault! If he hadn't been so disrespectful, he would've never had to teach him a lesson. Stupid man! He deserved what he got.

And it was Junelle's fault. If she didn't continue to ignore him and treat him as he deserved to be treated, none of this would be necessary.

Yes.

It was her fault.

All of it.

Perhaps it was time to teach her a lesson.

One she wouldn't forget. Where she'd understand he meant business. That she couldn't keep treating him this way.

Charles meowed, brushing his leg after downing his food in record time. One would think he didn't feed his cat in regular intervals the way Charles was acting.

He picked him up, rubbing his back.

"I think I have to call out today from work. You don't look so good. I think a visit to the vet is in order." He set Charles down and picked up his phone.

At least, that's what he'd tell his job. That he needed to take care of his cat.

Instead, he'd be taking care of something else. Something much more important.

Letting Junelle know that treating him with such disdain would not be tolerated.

JUNELLE PUSHED THE CART, trying to ignore the heated conversation Jason was having. Though it was difficult to do because he wasn't taking care to be very quiet. She turned the corner, heading down the cereal aisle, looking at the options but not really seeing anything. Her entire focus was on the angry words coming out of her brother's mouth.

One minute there were swear words filling the aisle, the next, silence coated the air.

She tore her gaze away from the boxes lining the shelves and toward her brother. He was breathing heavily, a vein bulging in his neck as he stared at his phone.

"Who was that?"

Jason looked up. "A client."

Her eyes widened as she threw a hand to her hip. "You were *not* speaking to a client that way. The amount of F bombs I heard..." Had her brother lost his mind?

He walked closer, his voice low and menacing. "And I'll throw a few more out if he tells me again to get my ass into work because your *little* problem is just that. A little problem that can be solved with a simple sorry. As if you're causing this issue. As if you know who's doing this and if you bowed down like a good little girl, it would all stop. Hell no. I'll rip up my contract with him before I bow down to his demands.

There are people working on his project. I don't need to be there, which is what I told him. And when I find out who told a client about my personal issues, they'll be fired."

Her breath clogged in her throat for a short second as his words echoed in her mind. She didn't doubt a client said such things. Some men were like that. Condescending and arrogant. A total asshole with no respect for anyone he deemed beneath him. Disgusting. She hoped Jason ripped up the contract anyway, to spite the man.

But Jason couldn't afford to lose money. Not because of her.

"You should—"

Jason held up his hand. "Don't finish that sentence, Junelle. No one speaks about you like that. No one. If he wants to fire my ass from the project, then that's his prerogative. But I'm not going to kiss his ass or allow him to talk about you like that. He's not the only client out there."

Maybe not, but she knew it had been a big contract he'd landed. Jason had been building his construction company since he graduated from college. He'd gone to school for finance and then chosen construction as his business. He was a very hands-on boss too. He loved working alongside his crew more than he liked being holed up in an office.

"Now, let's finish grocery shopping. Then we'll drop off the groceries and meet Tawney at the new gym. I want you to start learning how to defend yourself. Are we clear?"

She hated when her brother spoke to her like that. As if she had no brain and needed to be told what to do. But she decided to let it go because she knew why he was acting this way. Paul was dead and someone out there could hurt her as well.

Not trusting her voice though, she nodded and grabbed

a box from the shelf, not even caring what kind of cereal she grabbed.

They went through the rest of the store in silence. She got everything on her list and not a thing more. Jason didn't even grab anything extra, and he'd been known to do that, especially when she was buying the food. He was a junk food fanatic and never missed an opportunity to extort her for extra sweet treats.

The ride home continued in silence. Even bringing the groceries inside the house remained quiet. They put the food away as if they'd been roommates for the longest time, working in sync. She called Tawney to make sure they were still on before leaving once again. The ride to the gym was also filled with nothing said between them. She didn't know what to say.

She knew why Jason was upset with his client, but she hated to think he could lose the contract because of her. How long did he expect to not go into work? How long did he think his clients would let him get away with it? Some of them were very needy. So clingy that it boggled her mind. Grown-ass adults acting like they needed to be coddled like a child.

How long would she have to hide and have protection? She didn't want to think about it.

Tawney must've sensed the tension, but didn't comment on it. When Jason barked at her to pay attention and listen to everything Tawney said, she had to step between the two before Tawney did something she'd regret. Or more like he'd regret. Tawney wouldn't hold back if the need arose.

Then she leaned closer to her brother. "I get you're pissed, but why are you taking it out on me? What did I do wrong?"

Jason flinched as if she had slapped him. His mouth fell into a frown, his eyes filling with regret. "Shit, Junelle. You didn't do anything wrong. You're right. I am pissed, but not at you."

"Then stop acting like you are! Now go sit over there while I learn how to fight. If you don't knock it off, I'll use my newfound skills on you first."

Jason grinned at that, but listened.

Tawney cocked a brow, looking at her brother. "What's his problem?"

"I don't even know where to start."

Tawney stared at him for the longest time before looking at her. "Well I know where to start. I'm going to teach you how to take down a man and make sure he stays down. Hitting their nutsack is a surefire way to do so."

Junelle couldn't wait.

Tawney got right to work. For an hour and a half, they went from one move to the next, working up a sweat. By the time they were finished, Junelle hurt in every part of her body. But she felt a little bit more confident. Not completely where she thought she could take down a man—yet. But enough where she wouldn't panic.

The gym had a nice locker room. She and Tawney both showered before leaving. Tawney glared at Jason on her way out, and all she could do was chuckle at his wounded expression.

"Remind me never to get on her bad side."

That had more laughter coming out. "Umm, you idiot. You already have."

"Good point." Jason's laughter echoed as they stepped outside of the gym. "Remind me to not do it in the future then."

"As an apology, you can treat me to a late lunch. I'm starving, so make it a good place."

"You got it, sis. You know," Jason started, "I am—"

He grunted, bending when someone jumped out of a connecting street and pushed into his side.

"Hey..." The rest of her words slid away when she saw the knife in the man's hand.

She froze.

Before Jason could right his stance, the man jabbed Jason a few times. More groans slipped from his mouth.

She could do nothing but stare in horror. All that time in the gym had been for nothing. She was useless.

Jason dropped to the sidewalk.

The man who wore a ski mask, obscuring everything but his eyes and mouth, turned his attention to her.

Her entire body shook, yet remained immobile. No words escaped. Not a scream. Not even a whimper appeared.

"You needed to learn a lesson. Think on this and I'll be back. By then, you should know I demand respect."

Then the man dashed back down the street he'd come from.

It's as if the bubble she'd been thrust in burst. A flurry of activity was bouncing around her. People on their phones, calling the police. Two men were by Jason's side, pressing on his wounds.

"Jason!"

She dropped to her knees and grabbed his hand. "Stay with me. Please, Jason, stay with me."

His eyes were closed and she couldn't see his body lifting up and down as if he were breathing. He had to breathe! He had to!

"No. No. Jason." She looked up at the Good Samaritan

holding a jacket against his chest. "He's going to be okay. Right? He's going to be okay."

The man looked at her, bobbing his head up and down, but his eyes betrayed him.

Her brother wasn't going to be okay.

He wasn't even breathing.

10

HE CROSSED HIS ARMS, not even flinching at the deluge of words that hit him in his face. Rider would stand here for a few more minutes to let Cramer get everything off his chest and then he was going to continue doing his job.

They'd tried Roger's apartment first with no luck. Even spoke with a few neighbors who couldn't report anything odd. They didn't see Roger leave. In fact, they rarely saw the guy, and when they did, he wasn't very sociable. He'd been known to report other residents for noise complaints. They spoke to the landlord who confirmed the same. Roger was a quiet man himself, and he didn't tolerate other residents not showing the same courtesy.

From there, they went to the theater, hoping he had reported to work. Just their luck, he called out. Of all excuses, to take care of his sick cat. It blew his mind that the man owned a cat. What kind of person owned a pet, and then went and killed someone else's pet?

A truly sick bastard.

Rider doubted it the moment he heard it. So much so

that he wanted to return to Roger's apartment and make the landlord open his place up so he could verify the cat was gone. Or if he even owned a cat. Once he did that, his next move would be to find the vet he'd taken it to.

Finding Roger was his top priority. Listening to Cramer drone on and on about pissing on his case was wasting his time.

"Are you done yet?" Rider asked, interrupting Cramer mid-spiel.

Cramer looked ready to throw a punch. Stromberg, who stood next to him, stepped between them before he could. Rider would have welcomed it—and returned a few punches himself.

"We have a right to interview Mr. Woodson about why his car was spotted in a co-worker's neighborhood. A co-worker whose dog was murdered. A co-worker who's being stalked. Why did he have blood all over his person? We're not here because of Paul. Those are questions he needs to answer."

Cramer narrowed his eyes. "Why don't I believe you?"

Stromberg smiled. "I swear to you. I wouldn't lie."

Rider held in a snort. Stromberg would lie. He knew the truth to that now. Because the man had lied to him in the past, and that wasn't something he would've ever believed about him.

But Cramer must've taken his word because he backed up a few steps and nodded. "Fine. It better be about your case and your case alone. Otherwise, we're going to have issues." Then he walked away.

"If only he knew the truth."

Stromberg chuckled. "About?"

His brow rose in slow increments. "That you lie."

"Now, to be fair, I didn't technically lie. We aren't here about Paul. I didn't say we wouldn't bring up Paul's murder once we found Roger." Stromberg delivered a sly grin.

"I'm pretty sure Cramer isn't going to care about those kinds of semantics."

"Do you?"

He shook his head. "Hell no. I care about finding this asshole."

Tate had been talking to a few other employees while Cramer hollered at them for interfering. Although he never asked, Rider found it curious Jackson and Cramer even showed up at the theater again to interview the employees. They had thought it was a robbery gone bad with Paul's case. So why come back to where Paul worked?

They found Tate near the entrance talking on his phone. Tate slid the device into his pocket as they stopped next to him. The expression on his face didn't bode well.

"What's up? Abby again?" Stromberg asked.

Rider hadn't been paying complete attention in the car while driving around the city to each destination, but he had gotten the gist from their conversations and a few phone calls from Abby that they were disagreeing on where to take their late honeymoon. They had gotten married with little fanfare a month ago at the courthouse. That part didn't bother Abby, but she insisted on a true honeymoon. All-inclusive, somewhere tropical. Tate didn't mind that, but they weren't agreeing on the place yet. Such a ridiculous thing to argue about, but he wasn't going to voice the opinion.

"No, Officer Dorenson."

That jackass. He was one of the officers that thought it funny to have detectives respond to the body of a dog.

Stromberg scoffed and rolled his eyes. "Did you tell him to piss off? That we're busy."

Tate ignored his partner and looked at him. Rider wished he stood near a wall. He had the sudden feeling he'd need something to support him in a moment.

Tate must've sensed the same thing because he stepped closer and touched his shoulder. "We need to go to the hospital. Jason's been attacked. Junelle's unharmed."

He felt Stromberg's hand touch his other shoulder. He was supported by both his colleagues and yet his body felt like deadweight. One small movement and he'd crash to the floor.

"What happened?" The words barely came out in a whisper. As if his body was disengaged from everything, even his voice.

"Preliminary reports from Dorenson says they were leaving the gym and some random person walked up and stabbed Jason. Several times. The person never touched Junelle."

He appreciated the fact Tate kept mentioning Junelle was safe, but that didn't take away from the fact his best friend had been hurt. A man he thought of like a brother. A man he'd been pushing away from the moment he'd been reunited with him.

"Come on," Tate urged him, guiding him to walk forward with Stromberg's strength on his other side.

He had no idea how he made it to the car in one piece. His legs moved, but he was disconnected from everything. One moment they were driving, and the next Stromberg was telling him to get out of the car.

The walk inside the hospital was a blur. Nothing came into focus until he saw Junelle sitting in a chair by herself. When her tearstained face looked up and met his, all his senses came back to him. He rushed to her side, crushing her into his protective frame. He'd die before he let anything happen to her.

Her tears hit his shirt, soaking into his skin. A few of his own slid down his cheek, but he made no move to wipe them away. He held her for the longest time, rubbing his hand up and down her back, whispering comforting words. When he drew her away, he couldn't even remember what the hell he whispered.

The blood on her shirt gutted him. Eviscerated his heart into a million pieces. His best friend could be dead at this very moment. What had he done? Nothing. He wallowed in self-disgust for a whole day instead of working the case until he caught the bastard causing havoc in her life.

This was all his fault.

"He's in surgery."

Rider jerked at Stromberg's sudden voice in his ear. He turned toward him, tucking Junelle into his side. He wasn't ready to let her go. By the way she clung to him, she wasn't ready for that either.

"I swear he wasn't breathing. The whole time we waited for the ambulance, I didn't see his chest move at all," Junelle said, cries mingled with every word.

Rider didn't know what to say, so he focused his attention on Stromberg, who continued. "He was stabbed five times. All on his left side. He's in good hands here."

He knew that was meant to reassure him. It was the same hospital he'd been treated at. He survived two stab wounds—narrowly. But five? What were the odds?

Shit!

The last thing he wanted to do was upset Junelle further, but he couldn't think like a friend right now. He had to react like a detective.

Letting go of her waist, his hand reached for hers, grasping it. "June Bug...look at me."

She lifted her distraught face, the tears raining down. The look sent a wave of terror straight to his soul. He couldn't fail her. That's what he kept telling himself all last night and this morning and that's what he was doing. Failing her left and right.

Shoving that horrendous feeling aside, he forged on. "I need you to tell me what happened."

She shook her head and her hand got limp in his as if all her strength was depleted. He had no doubt it was, but he needed her to be strong for a little while longer.

"We were told someone came out of nowhere. Attacked right away. That Jason had no time to react and fight back."

Her eyes widened, nodding. Her mouth twisted, her chin quivering, but nothing but more tears came out.

"Did you get a good look at the person's face?" Because Rider knew in the pit of his stomach that Roger Woodson was the culprit. There was no damn sick cat!

"He...he wore a ski mask."

Well, he'd give Roger credit. He wasn't a complete idiot.

"I'm going to find who did this." Scratch that. Stromberg and Tate would. He was not leaving her side. For anything.

"He spoke to me."

Rider went rigid. "What did he say?"

"Something about how I needed to learn a lesson and to respect him." She shook her head, wrapping her arms around her stomach as if she had to protect herself. "That he'd be back."

"I'm not leaving you alone. You're safe. You're safe with me. I'll die before I let anyone hurt you." Then he pulled her back into his arms as her cries increased in volume, soaking his shirt once again.

He looked at Stromberg, not once loosening his hold on her. "I'm not leaving her. Go find this asshole now!"

"We're on it."

Then Stromberg and Tate left without looking back.

JUNELLE SET her bag down by the couch, looking around Rider's apartment, even though she already knew what it looked like. She'd been here a few times already. But it gave her something to do. Something to focus on.

They sat at the hospital all day long waiting on news of her brother. He made it out of surgery, though he was nowhere near out of the woods. Now he was in the ICU fighting for his life. He'd lost a lot of blood—too much— and the knife wounds had torn everything inside. The doctors had done what they could, and now it was up to her brother to fight the rest of the way. But that was her brother. Always fighting. And she needed him to keep fighting until he woke up.

When the doctor told her to go home and he'd call when there was news, she wanted to argue. Rider, who had been by her side the entire time, didn't let her. He made her leave, bringing her home. Then he told her to pack a bag, she was going to his apartment to stay. She didn't argue then either.

Now she stood in a place that was so unfamiliar yet made her feel safer than she had in the longest time.

"Hey, why don't you take a shower?" He looked down at her shirt that she had yet to change from the bloodstains and then back up to her face. His comforting smile encouraged her to follow directions more than anything else would've.

She walked as if on auto-pilot toward the bathroom. He

grabbed her a towel and washcloth and even turned on the faucet. Her clothes dropped to the floor, but she didn't even have the energy to throw them in the trash. But that's where they'd go when she found the nerve to do so.

Hot water hit her body, yet her muscles didn't work. She stood there, letting the water rain down on her. She thought she heard Rider call out her name. Maybe even knocked a few times on the door.

Nothing penetrated her fragile mind. Nothing but the image of her brother, bleeding out on the dirty sidewalk.

"Shit, June Bug, the water is freezing."

She turned to Rider, surprised to see him standing there. She hadn't heard the door open or the shower curtain whipped to the side when he moved it. He turned off the water, then grabbed the towel from the toilet seat where he had set it before walking out of the room earlier.

He wrapped it around her, holding it closed. "Did you even wash yourself?"

One quick shake was all she could manage. While she'd gotten wet from head to toe, she hadn't done anything but stand there.

"It's okay. I got you." Then he dried her off and helped her step out of the shower. Clothes—she wasn't sure where they came from because she hadn't bothered to bring her bag into the bathroom—sat on the counter. Rider took the white shirt and helped her put it on. He bent down and guided her feet into the pink underwear she didn't remember packing, pulling it up and covering her. Then he bent down again to help with the sweatpants. She figured she should feel embarrassed to be dressed like a child but not even that emotion could be conjured.

Before she could protest—not that she would've with her mind so detached—he scooped her up into his arms and walked down the short hallway to his room. The covers were already pulled back for him to set her down. Then he covered her up, placing a soft kiss on her forehead.

"Try to rest."

She grabbed his hand before he could walk away. "Don't leave me alone. Please, Rider. Don't leave me."

"Never, sweetheart. Never," he whispered in agony as he slid into the bed, pulling her into his arms.

She loved the fact he didn't even hesitate. He climbed into bed to comfort her and to give her what she wanted. If her brother wasn't clinging to the last threads of life, she'd jump with joy that she was back in Rider's arms. Something she never thought would be possible again.

She hid her head in his chest, gripping him so tightly that he'd have to fight her off if he wanted to get away. Her nails even dug into his back, no doubt making marks that would take days to fade. He didn't flinch once.

"I need to call my parents." Why hadn't she done that already?

"It's already taken care of." He smoothed his hand down her back, then up again. His legs were tangled with hers. His entire body a wall of protection, cocooning her from everything.

What else had he done while she'd been in her own little world? Crying and replaying the entire scene in her head.

"He's going to die, isn't he?"

Rider's embrace strengthened. "You know your brother. He doesn't give up easily."

Not a straight answer, and she knew why. Because Rider knew the truth. And the truth was her brother had a low chance of survival. She'd even seen it in the doctor's eyes when he spoke about her brother's condition. So much mumbo jumbo she couldn't remember all the terminology he'd spouted. Bottom line, her brother was on the brink of death.

"I feel like I'm dying myself, Rider. I feel empty inside." More tears rose to the surface, which was insane. She swore she'd emptied out every last drop she could in the hospital, she had cried for so long and so hard.

"I know, baby. I know. Me too. But I got you. You're safe."

She felt safe. With Rider next to her, she believed nothing could harm her. Yet, she had felt the same way with her brother. Look how that turned out.

When she trembled in his arms from the prospect of losing him as well, his arms tightened even more, crushing her. Even though it hurt, she didn't cry out in pain. She welcomed it because it meant she was alive. But for how long? There was a madman out there hurting people she knew and loved.

"I'm sorry I missed the last five years with you, but..."

"Shhh, June Bug. We're done talking about that. It doesn't even matter anymore."

She wiggled enough that he loosened his grip, allowing her to lift her head and look at him. "It does matter. Because to think I would've had to endure this kind of fear twice... when you were stabbed...I'm barely hanging on right now. To think..."

Rider brushed the top of her head, moving some strands of hair off her cheek. Then he kissed her forehead. "Stop thinking. Don't even go there."

"I can't lose him, Rider. I can't."

He winced, groaning. "I know, baby. I can't either. Just rest." He pressed his lips hard to her forehead, holding them there. "Close your eyes, June Bug. Don't think about it. I got you."

She let her head drop back to his chest, listening to his advice. "Don't leave me."

"Never. Never ever."

That was the last thing she remembered before falling into a restless sleep.

11

He didn't want to move from his spot. Even with his arm cramping from being under Junelle's body all night, the thought of moving eviscerated him. Those years she'd been gone from his life, he'd imagined moments like this. Tortured himself with the few memories he'd had with her. To have her back in his arms…he never wanted to let go.

But the reason for her in his bed and in his arms was not the way he wanted it. Jason was battling for his life, and he shouldn't even be thinking the things he was. Yet, he couldn't stop himself. Couldn't stop Junelle's pleas echoing in his mind. Don't leave her. How could he ignore that?

He couldn't. And he wouldn't, but he also needed to find the bastard who hurt Jason. Who wanted to hurt Junelle. Everything, from the moment she received the first threatening letter to Molly's death to Paul's murder to Jason's attack, it was all related. Same sick person out there wanting to harm the woman he loved.

His heart skipped a beat, causing the phantom pain to erupt in his chest. Instead of rubbing the spot, he bent his head, pressing a soft, tender kiss on her forehead.

He wouldn't ignore it anymore. He wouldn't pretend, not even to himself. Loving Junelle had never stopped. Not even once.

For that reason alone, he had a job to do.

"I love you, June Bug. So damn much," he whispered, before starting the painful process of pulling his arm out from underneath her.

It was a slow endeavor, having to stop and start when she'd shift or make a slight movement. She needed to rest, so he didn't want to risk waking her up.

After what felt like ages, he managed to free himself. Instead of retreating, he sat up, staring at her, hating to remove himself from the bed.

But if he didn't go now, he never would.

So with careful precision, he slid out of bed and adjusted the covers around her. Forgoing another kiss to her forehead—lest he wake her up—he walked out of the room, shutting the door without even making one sound.

His first task was to make coffee. It'd be a long day ahead of him and he needed all the caffeine he could get. After the coffee finished, he'd call Stromberg to get another update. He'd been in contact with them off and on yesterday. The moment he got into bed with Junelle, that had stopped. Morning had arrived and he couldn't hold back any longer. He needed to know what kind of progress they had made.

Yesterday, they had searched all over the city for Roger Woodson with no luck. Reluctantly, Cramer and Jackson had teamed up with them. Maybe it was due to the fact the last victim—damn, he hated to think of Jason in that sense, even though it was true—was his best friend. He'd thank Cramer and Jackson later for setting aside their irritation.

They had even gone over some of the security cameras on the block where Jason had been attacked, trying to follow the suspect's movements. There were a lot of security cameras and blocks to cover, so he wasn't sure if they had gotten anything from that yet.

He poured his coffee when a knock sounded on the door. A groan escaped when he looked through the peephole to see the last two people he had expected to see.

He opened the door, not even trying to hide his displeasure. "Bri. Abby," he stated, giving them both a pointed look that they should leave. Right this instant. When they did nothing but stare at him with smiles that made him damn nervous, he added, "How can I help you?"

"Oh, Rider," Bri said, offering a gentle smile, "it's not how you can help us. It's how we're going to help you."

Then she brushed by him as if he hadn't glared at them in a threatening manner. Abby strolled by too without even flinching.

He shut the door, locking it, before following them where they'd bolted to the kitchen, setting two large bags on the counter.

"What are you doing?"

Bri paused with her hand on a cupboard. "Finding your pans. We'll make breakfast while you shower."

"I'm not showering." At least, not yet. He had a phone call to make, which seemed like it should move up his list. Why the hell hadn't Stromberg or Tate warned him these two would drop by? Of course, maybe they knew he'd refuse such a visit and that's why they didn't tell him.

Abby shrugged, opening and closing cupboards as she said, "That's fine. You don't have to shower, but we thought you'd want one before you left."

Before he left?

He couldn't leave Junelle. Were they insane? While he wanted to help find Roger, he could do so from the comfort of his apartment. All he needed was access to the security cameras around the city. He'd take over that task or any other task he could from here.

"I'm not leaving."

They both stopped what they were doing, staring at him as if he was the one acting crazy. Wrong! They were the crazy ones.

Bri walked around the counter and stopped a few feet in front of him. "I'm sorry about your friend. Wyatt tells me that he's your best friend. That his sister is someone very important to you. I know it has to be killing you to be here and not out there looking for the asshole who hurt him."

Well, yeah. She wasn't wrong. But he still wasn't leaving Junelle alone. He'd gotten up to get ready to find the asshole, but again, not by leaving his apartment.

Abby appeared by Bri's side. "I know we don't know each other that well."

A short chuckle escaped. "I don't know either of you that well."

Sure, he might've seen Bri a bit more than Abby because of what happened in her apartment, but that didn't mean he *knew* her. They weren't friends or anything.

"You strike me as the kind of man who doesn't idly sit by and let others handle things," Abby continued.

What point was she trying to make? And again, she didn't know him, so why would she have that impression of him?

"Tate's the same way. Like, very annoying about it too at times." Abby rolled her eyes. "But I understand that sort of drive. That compulsion to do whatever it takes. Bri does too. Stromberg's the same way. That's why they make such good partners."

"I'm not leaving my apartment. Not while some madman

is out there hurting the ones I—" Well, love. But they didn't need to know his feelings he had for Junelle. He hadn't even told her himself. At least, not awake. "You two can leave."

Abby put her hand behind her back, then it reappeared, but this time not empty.

He took a step back.

She'd had a gun in her waistband. Now she held it in front of her, but thankfully not pointed at him as if she meant to threaten him to leave with the thing. What the hell! Did Tate know she carried a weapon around?

"I know how to handle this. In case you forgot, my brother was a serial killer. Not that he taught me how to murder a person, but we had a rough life growing up and I had to learn—he made sure of it—to protect myself. Your girlfriend is safe with me." Abby glanced at Bri. "With us."

Girlfriend?

While he knew his entire focus should be on the weapon in her hand, his mind centered on the one word—girlfriend.

If only.

Bri grabbed her purse she'd tossed on the couch and rummaged through it until she pulled out a taser. "I have this. I don't like guns. I'll leave that to Abby." Then she pulled out a can of Mace, a knife, and brass knuckles.

Abby giggled. "What is that?" She touched the brass knuckles, laughing some more.

Bri grinned. "I thought they looked neat when I saw them. I couldn't pass it up."

These women were insane. Confirmed now, the longer they were in his presence.

Then Bri turned the full-watt grin in his direction. "We might not look like we can protect anyone," her grin dimmed a little bit, but the fire remained in her eyes, "and I don't want to point it out, but I did protect myself from a killer. I don't go anywhere without a knife since that day. It makes me feel safer. It confirms to myself that I can and will protect myself if the need arises."

Yeah, he didn't like that reminder either. It pointed out his failure in protecting her. But she also wasn't wrong. She had defeated the asshole that wanted to kill her with her own two hands.

"We're not defenseless women. We'll make sure your girlfriend is safe," Abby said, tucking the gun behind her back again. "You might not want to admit it out loud, but you're dying to leave and find this asshole. I know you are. Because you're like Stromberg and Tate, even if you don't want to admit it."

Maybe he did want to leave. But he couldn't. If something happened to Junelle...he'd never forgive himself.

"We'll put a chair under the door for further resistance," Bri said, pointing to the front door. "We'll block the window to the fire escape as well. I promise you, she will be safe."

He flinched when a warm hand slid into his. He turned his head to the left to see Junelle standing right next to him. Her eyes were red-rimmed from all the crying the day before, but it didn't detract from her beauty. She was the most gorgeous woman on the planet. She always would be to him.

"I'll be okay, Rider. I need you to find this person. It's okay to leave. Don't let him get away with hurting Jason."

"I don't know if I can. I'm terrified." That confession came out in a throaty whisper.

Junelle touched his chest, pressing hard. "Me too. I know I said don't leave me last night, but I take it back. I need you to leave."

His mind took those words and warped them into something he knew she didn't mean. Leave for good. But maybe they were all right. He should leave. If he stayed, he'd let the fear for her consume him. What kind of protector would he be if he wasn't in his right mind?

"Find this bastard and make him pay. Please."

He nodded, relenting. "I'll go take a shower."

Then he walked away, feeling like he'd taken a huge blow to the gut. Somehow, he woke up feeling happy—despite the intense situation—and now he was back to being the saddest man on earth.

This erratic tug-of-war on his emotions was going to break him at some point.

———

Junelle watched Rider walk away and then disappear. She stared at the hallway a little longer than necessary before turning her attention to the two women. She hadn't heard the entire conversation between the three, but she'd heard enough. They were right. Rider would be dying to leave to find the person who hurt Jason, but he wouldn't because of her. That was unacceptable. That person had to pay!

"I'm Bri," the woman she recognized from the precinct the other day said, then pointed to the woman next to her. "This is Abby. She's married to Tate, or Detective Powell is probably how you know him. I'm engaged to Wyatt—Detective Stromberg. We're sorry about your brother."

Tears were rising to the surface again, and crying was the last thing she wanted to do. She'd done enough of that the last few days. Her head bobbed in a yes motion, but she felt disconnected from her body. Too many emotions circling her and it was making her dizzy.

"The hospital he's at is one of the best. He's in good

hands," Bri added, frowning, as if she knew she was mucking it up. Not that Junelle thought she was. Her positivity helped to hold the devastation she felt rising to the surface at bay.

"And if he doesn't make it, we're the perfect people to help you through it. Because we know what it feels like."

Junelle's eyes widened at Abby. What an odd thing to say. One woman bringing positivity with the other one spouting negativity. Maybe she shouldn't have told Rider to leave her with these women.

Even Bri looked at Abby as if she had lost her mind.

Abby grimaced, then shrugged. "That sounded...rude. I meant...I lost my brother. In fact, Tate and Stromberg killed him."

Junelle didn't think her eyes could bug out any more than they already were, but they felt like they'd spring right out of her face soon.

"It's a whole story. He killed a lot of people, but he wasn't a bad guy." Abby lips twisted in a cringe-like manner. "I mean yes, killing people is bad, but what I meant was he wasn't..." She sighed. "I'll never be able to explain what I mean. Bottom line, my brother loved me and would've done anything for me. I loved him in return. Losing him was hard. Then you have Bri here." Abby jabbed a finger in her direction. "Her sister was brutally murdered by a psychopath who tried to kill Bri as well. That's how Rider got hurt. Poor man can't get over the guilt of not being able to help. But that's a whole other conversation as well. So, what I'm getting at is we have both lost a sibling and we're here for you. For whatever might happen."

Abby smiled as if that would erase all the horrifying things she had said. "I'll go start breakfast." Then she swiveled around and bee-lined it for the kitchen.

Bri stepped closer, lowering her voice. "She meant well with everything she word-vomited. She can be intense sometimes, which isn't surprising because Tate can be too. It's Junelle, right?"

She shook her head at first—more so to clear her head of everything that happened—but then realized what she did and nodded. "Yes, it's Junelle. I appreciate you both coming here. As much as I hate to see Rider leave, I want him to find this guy."

"He will. All three of them together will. They can be very determined men when they want to be. Come on." Bri tossed her head for Junelle to follow, and she did.

Rider didn't have stools for the counter separating the kitchen from the living room, so she stood there while the women worked in tandem. As if it weren't the first time they mingled together in the kitchen. What a history report she had been given. She had so many questions now, but it felt awkward to ask any.

Bri set a glass of orange juice in front of her with a gentle smile. "A mimosa. If you're not a drinker, I'll drink it for you."

No way in hell. She hoped it was strong.

She produced her first smile of the morning as she wrapped her hand around the glass. "Thank you."

"So, how long have you been dating Rider?" Abby's brows rose, the glee in her expression to hear the whole story.

"Umm..." Where to start? Well, Abby had been honest with her, so why should she hold back? "We're not dating. We haven't for a very long time. I sort of messed it up with him."

Abby glanced at her, then back at the eggs she was

frying. "Details. We need details. Because that man did *not* correct me when I called you his girlfriend."

Oh, she didn't hear that part.

Why didn't he correct her?

She heard the bathroom door open, twisting to see if Rider was coming this way. When he didn't appear, she turned back toward them.

Bri winked. "We'll get the scoop once he leaves."

Abby shared a look with Bri and offered a tilt to her head that she understood.

Rider joined them a few short minutes later looking refreshed and oh so handsome. He'd trimmed his beard, and it made her want to smooth her hand over it, just to feel the texture. His hair, which was a bit shaggy and had been in all different directions before the shower, was now combed over to the left. The sides were cut short with the top of his head holding longer hair. He parted his hair on the side, sweeping the long strands into a nice arch that she wanted to mess up and put back into the wildness it had been earlier. He wore a black suit with a bright-blue shirt that brought out the color of his gorgeous baby-blue eyes. Why did he have to look so damn good?

Somehow, some way she needed to earn his trust back. Get them to where they were before she ruined everything.

He looked at Abby and Bri, but didn't say anything. Though the hardness in his gaze said enough. At least to her it did. He didn't like anything that was going on. Then he turned his attention to her, eliciting the most radiant smile she'd seen yet from him. Oh, how she wanted to hold him tight and kiss him until he changed his mind and they stayed in—preferably in his bed.

That sudden thought horrified her. Her brother was

lying in a hospital bed, near death, and she was having lustful thoughts of Rider.

"Hey," he whispered, leaning closer, placing a hand on her waist. "What's wrong?"

Everything! I'm having immoral thoughts!

"Nothing. I'm worried about Jason."

Liar! She was worried about Jason, but that hadn't been what she'd been thinking.

"Me too. I called the hospital a little bit ago and he's hanging in there. He hasn't gotten better, but he hasn't gotten worse. So I consider that good news."

"Yes, it is."

That beautiful smile he wore disappeared. Now nothing but a sad, dejected look remained. "I know you want to go see him, but please stay here. Don't leave for anything. I'll be back as soon as I can."

While she wanted to argue with him, she knew he was right. It wasn't safe to leave. Look at what happened to Jason. In broad daylight. It happened so fast, neither one of them had been able to fight back.

"I won't."

He leaned closer, this time putting his other hand on her cheek. "Promise me. I can't leave if I'm worrying about you."

She licked her lips. His eyes trained on the movement, inhaling a sharp breath.

"I promise."

Then she licked her lips again. His hand tightened on her waist as did the one on her cheek. His jaw clenched, a muscle darting in and out.

She wasn't the only one with lustful thoughts on her mind. Good to know.

Her tongue slid out to do another swipe when he leaned so close she felt his breath on her lips.

"Stop it, June Bug."

"I'm not doing anything." She couldn't resist producing a wicked grin.

"You know what you're doing, and you're making it a hundred times harder to leave." He rested his forehead against hers. "I'll call you later."

She didn't know where her phone was, but she couldn't find the strength to ask—not with him so close to her.

Then he kissed her hard on the forehead before stepping away. "Keep her safe."

He was gone before she could get another word in.

Both women converged in her space.

"First story time, then we eat." Abby waved a hand in front of her face like she was hot. "Because I need details now. I was praying in my head he'd kiss you and the man disappointed me. The damn forehead doesn't count."

Funny. It disappointed her beyond reason as well.

Not once last night while in bed with him had she thought about kissing him. Now, all she wanted to do was that...and so much more.

12

———

After showering, getting dressed and ready, he'd made a few phone calls. One of them had been to Stromberg for an update and a location of where to meet him. It didn't take long for him to get to Roger Woodson's apartment. Tate, Stromberg, Cramer, and Jackson were all in the lobby when he arrived.

He gave his heartfelt thanks to Cramer and Jackson and brushed off their sympathies for Jason. Hearing that kind of shit would drive home his best friend was fighting for his life. He didn't want to think about it, so therefore he didn't want to hear anything about it.

They hadn't gotten any good views on the security cameras from the attack. Roger—assuming he was their perp—had kept his face hidden behind the ski mask for the longest time. The suspect had jaunted down several blocks, never keeping to a straight path before he had dipped into one of the subway entrances and slipped onto one without giving away his identity. Confirming who it was wouldn't be as easy as he hoped.

"Did the judge sign the warrant?" Rider asked Cramer.

That was the other thing Stromberg had mentioned. They wanted to search Roger's apartment, so Cramer and Jackson had gone to a judge for a warrant.

Cramer shook his head, his lips grim.

It had been a long shot. There wasn't much evidence to give them probable cause to get inside his place. But if they could, it might provide another avenue to look for him. Yesterday, according to Stromberg, they'd come up empty everywhere. They'd even contacted the theater this morning. Roger didn't show up for his shift, or even call in that he wouldn't be working today.

The man was on the run.

Which confirmed his suspicions. He was their perp.

"But I knocked on the building superintendent's door and asked if we could look around his place. Sort of a wellness check," Tate said with a wicked grin.

"You're all standing around," Rider pointed out. "Does that mean the answer was no?"

Stromberg shrugged. "He said he had to make a call first. We're waiting for him to come back."

Rider glanced at the group, unable to suppress a tired grin. "He's not going to believe we're conducting a wellness check. It doesn't take five detectives to do something like that."

"True," Tate said, his cocky grin still displayed. "But we are also concerned about his cat. Since no one has heard or seen Mr. Woodson all day yesterday—besides the one phone call to his job about taking his cat to the vet—or this morning, we are concerned about his pet. I also pressed upon to Mr. Delgati, the super, that he should also be concerned about that. Who knows what a cat could get up to on its own for a long period of time. No one to feed it. No one to change the kitty litter."

Jackson chuckled. "He *really* impressed upon it. I was even starting to get ready for what the cat has done unattended."

They waited a few more minutes before Mr. Delgati walked back into the lobby. While he walked with an easy-going step, his irate expression didn't bode well.

"I'm sorry, gentlemen. I'll be unable to open Mr. Woodson's door for you. I confirmed with the local precinct, no missing person's report has been filed for Mr. Woodson, therefore I doubt your story about wanting to do a wellness check."

Now Rider wanted to know what kind of story Tate had given him.

Mr. Delgati continued. "Furthermore, Mr. Woodson does not own a cat. I checked our records and he's never had a cat."

Rider opened his mouth to argue that point, but Tate beat him to it. "He has a cat, Mr. Delgati. Perhaps you should double check that because if your records state he doesn't, and we heard he does, well, he's in violation of his rental agreement. Now isn't he?"

Mr. Delgati looked pensive. "How do you know this information?"

"It's my job to know this kind of information. He called out of work yesterday to take his cat to the vet. This morning, he didn't even call in to work. He just didn't show up. His employer is very concerned about his well-being. I doubt his boss thought to file a missing person's report yet. But I will advise him to do so as soon as we leave here. If he doesn't have a cat, then that's even more concerning. We have reason to believe he wants to harm...himself."

Rider nearly chortled at that. Tate almost told the truth.

Roger didn't want to harm himself. He wanted to harm everyone else.

The anger Mr. Delgati walked out with disappeared, replaced with uncertainty.

"Mr. Delgati, we respect your decision and the rules of this apartment complex. We only want to make sure Mr. Woodson isn't in trouble. We can all wait downstairs while you take a quick peek to see if he even has a cat. Because if he has a cat—something he shouldn't—then it's best animal control is called. Or whatever the stipulation is for having a pet without prior approval." Tate made sure to maintain his smile, but Rider noticed he'd dropped the smugness from it. He had to admit, Tate had a way with words. He was buying all this crap flying out of his mouth.

And if animal control was called, maybe one of them would be able to pop into the apartment with them. They all didn't need to step inside.

"Well, I can't argue with that. If he has a cat..." Mr. Delgati shook his head, his anger flaring back to life. "We go through a rigorous process when it comes to pets. Some people have no respect for property. Cats are the worst. I'll be right back."

Mr. Delgati left the room with hurried steps.

"Nice job, Tate," Cramer said, though his facial expression said he had to force the compliment out.

"I always get what I want," Tate replied with a shit-eating grin. "Always."

Then Tate looked at him. Rider could see in the depths of his gaze that Tate meant he would've gotten into that apartment one way or another. Even by illegal means. He did things by the book. He believed in the law, in right from wrong. But right now, with this situation, nothing mattered but getting this asshole before he hurt someone else—especially Junelle.

Mr. Delgati came back into the room with the fire blazing to dangerous depths in his eyes. "He has a damn cat! The mongrel hid from me. I will be calling animal control."

Tate feigned shock. "I'm so sorry that Mr. Woodson lied to you."

He wasn't shocked by the development at all. What was one tiny lie about owning a cat when he had murdered a human being. Hell, he had killed a dog too. Rider knew with every fiber of his being that Roger was behind it all. Why kill a dog but own a cat? He figured someone who could kill a defenseless animal would hate all creatures.

"Obviously, Mr. Woodson isn't in the residence," Tate prodded, continuing the worried detective act.

They all knew he wouldn't be there. He was on the run. Hiding from the police would be his main objective.

"Not that I saw. My mind was focused on the cat. Once I saw the beast, I didn't check the rest of the rooms." Mr. Delgati cleared his throat. "If you want to take a quick peek, be my guest. Grab the cat too."

Tate beamed his most winning smile at Mr. Delgati, thanking him as the super handed over the key.

Rider couldn't believe their luck had turned. And all because of a cat. He also got the impression that Mr. Delgati didn't approve of pet owners in general. He'd bet his life savings not many people got permission to have one in their residence.

They made their way to Roger's apartment. Tate unlocked the door and they all filed in. The place was tidy, for the most part. A few dishes on the counter, but otherwise the kitchen was spotless. The living room didn't have many knickknacks. A small TV sat on a stand with no DVDs or any kind of cable box around it. Did Roger not like to watch anything? Though there was an internet modem, so maybe he streamed services to watch his shows.

Cramer and Jackson headed down the hallway to the bedroom at the end. Tate popped into the bathroom. He and Stromberg walked into the first bedroom. A desk sat in the corner with a lamp sitting on it. Nothing cluttered the top of it. The closet doors were closed. Besides the sparseness of the room, the thing that stood out was the large freezer against the wall. For a single man, it seemed over the top. But maybe he didn't like shopping all the time and stocked up for a long haul. It was odd. And it needed to be checked.

He and Stromberg shared a look, thinking along the same lines before he walked up to it and flipped the lid up.

A shocking shiver slid down his spine as he stared at the dead body.

"Well, shit. I didn't expect that," Stromberg mumbled under this breath.

"Nothing in the bathroom, and I can hear Cramer and Jackson digging around the room. What's in there?" Tate asked, then strolled up next to him, inhaling a sharp breath. Looking had answered his own question. "What the hell? That looks like..."

Like Roger Woodson.

While the body was frozen to the bone, they could make out the man's features. It looked like the same man from the driver's license he'd printed just yesterday morning.

None of this made sense.

"Room's clean. Not much in there besides clothes. This guy really doesn't keep knickknacks or anything," Jackson said as he strolled into the room.

"It doesn't matter. Woodson's not our guy." Rider threw a frustrated hand toward the freezer.

Because if he was dead in the freezer, he couldn't have killed anyone.

Jackson shook his head as he took a peek in the freezer. "That's not Woodson."

"Excuse me?" Rider asked. Of course it was. It was the same man from the driver's license photo. He'd bet his life on it. "I got a match for the plates from the video we received related to my case I'm working on. Those plates belong to Roger Woodson. I printed out his driver's license photo yesterday. This is him."

Jackson pointed at the body. "If you're saying that man is Roger Woodson, then I don't know who the hell we interviewed the other day at the theater claiming to be Woodson. Because it wasn't that guy."

Holy. Shit. What the hell was going on?

Rider wasn't even sure he wanted to know. Because it didn't negate the fact Junelle was still in danger. From a complete psychopath.

STUPID. Stupid. Stupid.

He should've gotten Charles before he left yesterday. Though after stabbing the meddling brother, he had every intention to return home. Despite gutting that despicable man at close quarters and keeping the jabs one right after another, it had been a messy endeavor. Blood had spattered onto his clothes and hands. He'd been prepared for that. Wearing black clothes helped to conceal the color red. The ski mask had been a last-minute purchase. Of course, he made sure to purchase it clear across the other side of the city. No need to make things easy on the police. They'd never find out where he'd bought it. And it was a generic ski mask—there'd be no way to trace it even if he bought it close-by.

His steps had been surefooted, but easygoing. Running would attract more attention. Wearing the ski mask as long as he had had drawn enough attention on its own, especially since spring had sprung.

But he got away.

Without one person stopping him. Because that was the thing about most people, they didn't want to step in and help. They didn't want to risk themselves getting hurt in the process. Weak! The lot of them.

After getting on the subway, he got off and got back on a few more until he'd made sure his trail had been so unrecognizable they'd be running in circles for days trying to keep up with his movements.

Then he checked into a sleazy hotel that accepted cash and no identification, washing up before trying to decide what his next move would be. It should've been getting Charles before the police came sniffing around, but then he had decided it was too risky. The moment they showed up at the theater asking questions about Paul's death, he knew it would only be a matter of time.

And things had been going so well for him. He thought this time it would've been different. A new start. A new location. New people to meet.

But it was always the same.

Nobody treated him with respect.

He adjusted the sunglasses on his face before turning away from the apartment building he had called home for the longest time. Sticking around was too risky. The swarm of police vehicles that kept growing in numbers could be his downfall. He'd never let that happen.

They had found the body in the freezer.

The jig was up.

Well, it would be soon. They still had to figure out who was in the freezer. Once they did, it would make their jobs harder. All in all, he was still in the clear. They wouldn't catch him. Not unless he wanted to be caught, and he didn't want that to happen.

He'd take care of Junelle—that bitch needed to learn her lesson—and then he'd move on. Try a new spot. Start all over again like he did so many times before.

There was a lesson in every mistake. He'd learned several this time around. So that meant he wouldn't make them again.

The big question he had now was where had Junelle disappeared to? He'd driven past her house last night twice, not wanting to risk too much attention on himself. Both times, the house had remained dark. She had fled to somewhere else. Perhaps the police had stashed her somewhere.

But where?

Attacking her brother had been an impulsive move. He hadn't put much planning into it once he had made the decision he needed to be eliminated. And, of course, getting away without being caught had been the most important thing at the time. So he didn't follow Junelle's movements.

Unfortunate, but necessary.

An obstacle.

And if there was one thing he was good at, it was over-coming obstacles.

SHE WINCED when the toothbrush jammed into her gums. Tears built as her upper gum throbbed. She would *not* cry over this. Blood mingled with the peppermint toothpaste.

With her luck, she'd throw up next. Spitting out the disgusting mixture, she then went back to brushing her teeth, albeit more carefully this time.

After eating breakfast with Abby and Bri—and having two mimosas—Junelle retreated into the bathroom, claiming she wanted to shower. Of course, she did want to cleanse herself, but she also needed a break from the two women. While they were very cordial and understanding, they were also a lot to deal with. They bombarded her with too many emotions, coming from all angles. It was hard to maintain her composure. The last thing she wanted to do was lose her shit in front of people she didn't know.

Her tongue rubbed against the scrape on her gum, hoping to soothe it some, but it did nothing to ease the pain. Gritting her teeth with her lips wide, looking like a horse trying to smile, she stared at the wound. She'd hit the upper gum on the right side. While it was red with a noticeable scratch, the bleeding had stopped. It was nothing in the grand scheme of things. Not when her brother was fighting for his life from multiple stab wounds.

A terrifying shiver rushed down her spine as that thought entered her mind. Now wasn't the time to go down that path. The tears would start and then she'd embarrass herself in front of her visitors.

She finished getting ready, forgoing blow drying her hair, and went to Rider's room first. There was nothing she needed to do in the room, but she needed another minute to herself. She picked up her phone from the nightstand, noting no new texts or calls had come in. Even though Rider had called the hospital—and told her what they said—she'd called herself before jumping in the shower. Nothing new to report when she called either. Like Rider had said, no new news was good news.

Deciding she'd delayed long enough, though her emotions weren't back in sync yet, she returned to the living room where Bri and Abby were lounging on the couch. A quick glance at the kitchen said they'd cleaned up the mess from breakfast. The room went deadly silent when she entered. Not even the TV was on.

Rider had a couch with no other furniture besides the dining table with chairs to sit on.

"Come," Bri said with a gentle smile, as she moved over closer to Abby and patted the free space next to her.

Not wanting to make it awkward, she sat down.

They'd already grilled her on her past relationship with Rider. While any other time she might've wanted to delve deeper into it, she had kept it short and sweet. The basics of everything that went down. They'd nodded and given a few sympathies, but in the end, they hadn't said much. Because she'd been in the wrong and they knew it too.

They probably also had decided she wasn't good enough for Rider. It was something she had said to herself quite a bit since she had learned her mistake. She'd let a good man go because she wasn't mature enough to have an adult conversation. Because a simple talk about it all would've solved everything. She wouldn't have lost five years with a wonderful man.

Maybe they knew the turmoil she was going through in her mind because nobody spoke. Or maybe they didn't know what to say to her. Either way, the silence was awkward and stilted. She wanted to flee to Rider's room, but she didn't know what kind of excuse to use. Would it even matter the reason? She shouldn't have to make company with people she didn't know.

"Is it too soon to talk strategy?" Abby asked after what felt like an hour, but only a few minutes had passed.

Junelle's eyebrows dipped. Even Bri gave Abby a quizzical look.

Abby giggled. "How Junelle is going to jump Rider's bones."

Bri snort-laughed, then covered her mouth to stop the sound.

Junelle had to admit, she had a hard time stopping a chuckle from leaving her mouth. But she resisted—barely.

"I don't think..." Her face heated with embarrassment. She never was one who enjoyed confrontation. And while this wasn't enemy territory kind of confrontation, it was still a conversation she wished she could avoid. "I'm not sure he'd appreciate that."

"Sometimes it's not about what a man will appreciate, but what he needs." Abby's lips twisted into a devious smirk. "They'll be the last to admit what they need from you."

Bri nodded, as if agreeing with Abby's assessment. "While he could've done better than a kiss to the forehead, it *was* still a kiss. That means something."

Abby murmured in agreement. "He must think it's too soon to jump your bones. So therefore, you need to eliminate the question lingering between you two and do it."

She blinked several times. One, to get her bearings down. Two, because she had no idea how to respond. Her, make the first move. She couldn't even do that five years ago. She'd kept her crush hidden from him until he revealed his own.

When it came to the game of love, she was a first-class loser. In every round. Her colossal mistake was proof of that.

"I can't."

Abby cocked a brow. "You can." She said it with such conviction, as if no one ever disagreed with her.

"No, really, I can't. I wasn't even the first one to make a

move back then. I don't have...the confidence." It hurt to admit that, but it was the truth.

"Well," Bri said, putting a light hand on her shoulder, "no one's going to make you do anything you don't feel comfortable with." Bri glanced at Abby as if warning her to drop it. "But I do believe that if you made your feelings known, Rider wouldn't hesitate to reciprocate. He didn't say what he was feeling this morning, but the intensity in his eyes said enough. He cares about you."

"Yes, yes, everything Bri said is true." Abby huffed, slouching into her spot as if she'd been defeated in a battle she thought she'd win. "I was trying to fill the silence. Now what should we talk about?"

That had Junelle giggling, unable to hold that one in. "After that topic, I don't think it can get much worse."

Abby smiled, her posture regaining a bit of life. "How about we make some cookies or something? I know keeping busy can help stop the mind from wandering." Abby leaned forward and her hand twitched as if she wanted to reach out like Bri had. But she was too far away to do it and not appear awkward in the endeavor. "I know you're worried about your brother, and rightly so. I'm sorry if my comments were inappropriate. I didn't mean to be rude."

Junelle didn't hold it against her. She understood what Abby had tried to do, and she appreciated it.

"It's okay. Baking cookies sounds like a good idea. Another mimosa to go with it." Maybe after a few more drinks, she'd want to talk strategy. Because getting Rider back in her life—permanently—was a goal of hers. She'd blocked him out of her mind for so long, it had become routine. It hadn't taken much effort to let him back in. Now that he was in her life, she didn't want to lose him again.

13

JUNELLE PAUSED in scooping a cup of flour, listening. Her phone was going off. She'd left it in Rider's room.

"I should get that." She dropped the measuring cup in the flour container and walked out of the room before either woman could argue. Not that they had a reason to argue about something so trivial.

Maybe the ladies knew Rider wouldn't be prepared for any kind of baking, because they had brought two large bags with them. The cupboards had been sparse of the ingredients they needed. Which hadn't surprised Junelle. Rider had never been the baker type of guy, and she didn't think that had changed in the last five years. It was nice to know they had come prepared to distract her.

When she picked up the phone, seeing her mom's number on the screen, she wished she had ignored the ringing and continued to bake.

"Hey, Mom."

"Where are you?" her mom screeched, then she took a few deep breaths before continuing. "We just made it to the hospital. Are you in the cafeteria? I could use a coffee. The flight was so long and exhausting."

Shit! Her parents had flown home from Italy, which she knew they would when Rider said he'd called them. But she had never asked for any other details about them. When would they arrive? Had Rider known and decided not to tell her? How much did he tell them about what was going on?

"I'm...I'm not there. I'm at Rider's."

"Oh." Her mom paused for a long time, as if trying to find the right words. "I was surprised when he called us and not you."

And she was grateful he had the foresight to call them when she'd shut down completely.

"I didn't realize Jason was talking to Rider again," her mom continued when she didn't respond to her last comment.

Where did she start to explain?

How could she explain Jason had gotten hurt because of her?

Would her mom understand why she couldn't come to the hospital? That it wasn't safe for her?

"Junelle? Talk to me. I need you here."

She couldn't deny her mother that. Even if it wasn't safe. Her parents needed her, and she needed them.

"I'll be right there."

Then she hung up before her mom tried to bombard her with more questions that she didn't know how to answer.

She grabbed a sweatshirt and threw it on, then shoved her phone inside her purse and slung it over her shoulder. The moment the ladies saw her dressed as such, she knew she wouldn't have to explain where she was going. It was a blessing she didn't know she needed. To be understood without having to speak. To have comfort when she didn't know she desperately ached for it.

Abby shoved the cold ingredients into the fridge while Bri turned off the oven. Then they met her by the couch.

"You're not going alone." Abby pulled the gun she had from behind her waistband. "I'll protect you. I won't let this asshole get near you."

Bri smiled as she pulled a knife from behind her back. "Sameies."

That had a chuckle escaping. It went from quiet laughter into silent tears. "I don't know what to say to my parents."

Abby shook her head as she stepped closer and wrapped an arm around her shoulder. "You don't have to say anything to them. We can handle it for you. You're not alone in any of this."

These women didn't know her. She didn't know them. But she felt like she'd gained two best friends out of nowhere. It was a feeling she'd never forget.

"Here." Bri had put the knife back where she'd had it and produced a can of Mace. "Keep this on you. If you want something else to protect you, we'll get it."

She stared at the can until her eyes blurred. Would she have to use it? Then she found herself moving for the door, the women following her when she stopped and twirled around. "I should call Rider."

"Umm, no," Abby said sharply, guiding her to continue by pushing on her back. "With these men, you ask for forgiveness, not permission. And calling him would be like asking for permission. He'll tell you no, you'll say yes regardless. It'll turn into an argument. It's better to avoid all that. Text when we arrive at the hospital if you want."

The look on Bri's face said she agreed with everything

Abby said, so she continued toward the door without further resistance.

It didn't take too long to get to the hospital. They'd decided on getting a cab and avoiding the subway. Too many people, too many ways for someone to attack them. Junelle wished it would've taken longer. Because the longer she delayed, the more time she'd have to come up with the right words for her parents.

Her mom rushed to her side the moment she walked into the ICU waiting area. Her dad joined in on the fierce hug a few seconds later. They stood there holding each other, no one saying a word. Though she knew silent tears were raining down all of their cheeks.

When they parted, her mom zeroed in on Abby and Bri. "Who are your friends? Where's Rider?"

This was one reason she didn't want to come. Her mother would be relentless in her questioning. She wouldn't stop until she was satisfied, and even then, she'd keep asking questions and making statements because she hated silence. The TV or some kind of music was always on in the house for background noise.

Junelle made quick introductions and tried to avoid answering the other question as long as she could. It didn't last long.

"Mom, let's have a seat."

Her mom crossed her arms, her eyes taking on a fiery gaze while her lips thinned into a straight line. "I'll stand, thank you."

"Jason's hurt because of me." There. She said it. She spoke the words that had been filtering through her mind from the moment he hit the pavement, blood gushing out of his side and chest.

The ire in her mother's expression lessened, replaced

with confusion. Her dad stepped closer to her mom, putting an arm around her. "Come, Janice, let's take a seat."

She wanted to hug her dad. He was always the peace-keeper in the family, calming everyone down. He had the same questions in his expression as her mother did, but he maintained his composure, wanting Junelle to take it all at her own pace.

They sat down. Her parents on one side, with her, Abby, and Bri sitting across from them.

Her mouth started moving, words coming out, yet her mind felt detached from her body. She didn't leave anything out. Not Molly's murder, the letters, the horrible news of Paul's death. Nothing was left out even though she wanted to skirt some of the truth. Through it all, her parents' eyes grew larger and larger as it all sunk in.

When she finished, icky silence filled the area. She'd rendered her mom speechless for the first time in her life.

"So Rider's out looking for this man?" her mom asked, then nodded. "Yes, he'll find him. I know he will," she finished, answering her own question. Then she turned her attention to Abby and Bri. "Thank you, ladies, for coming with my daughter."

"Of course," Bri said. "Anything you need, we're here for all of you."

From there, her parents took control of the conversation —more like her mother—while she got lost in her own thoughts. What was Rider doing? Did he find the person yet? Would her brother make it? How long would she need protection?

A quiet ringtone startled her out of her musings. She dug her phone out, cringing when she saw the caller.

Abby hissed and winced, then chuckled. "You got this."

Bri's offer of support was a quick squeeze of her shoulder.

"It's Rider," she said, standing up with a short smile to her parents. Then she walked to a quiet corner far away from everyone and answered.

"Hey, I hope you have good news." Because she sure didn't. Maybe she didn't have to tell him where she was.

"Not really." He sounded tired and defeated. "How are you?"

"Okay."

"I called the hospital again. Still no news."

She gestured she knew that, then realized he couldn't see her—or that she'd gotten her own update when she arrived at the hospital. "I know." Short and sweet. If she didn't speak too much, he'd never find out she left his apartment.

"I might..." He hesitated, and she hated hearing it. She'd never known him to be unsure of himself. "I might be gone all day long. If Abby or Bri need to leave, I'll have someone else come there. I don't want you alone."

"I'll be fine. Don't worry about me." Absurd to say, but she had to anyway. By his huff, she knew he disregarded it without thought.

"I don't want you alone for even a moment."

"They won't leave me alone, Rider. Please don't worry about that."

There was a moment of silence.

"What are you three doing?"

Damn. He had to ask. Now she had to decide if she went with the truth and got it out of the way, or lied so he could keep his focus on finding the asshole who hurt Jason.

"Junelle?" He sighed. "What are you doing right now?"

He knew.

She sensed it right away that he knew they left.

———

Why wasn't she answering him?

Because she knew he wouldn't like the answer.

She left the apartment.

"Damn it, June Bug!" The words came out in a roar. He had to inhale and exhale a few breaths before continuing. "You promised me you wouldn't leave. You said the words I promise. So you tell me right now if you just broke that promise. Please tell me you didn't."

More silence filtered through the phone. Anger rose in his chest. Then it morphed into fear when the body they'd found in the freezer was rolled out of the door in a body bag.

She left while a madman was out hunting for her. What the hell had she been thinking?

"I guess silence is enough of an answer. Why am I surprised you couldn't keep that promise?"

The moment those words came out he wanted to retract them. Bringing up the past, even in a subtle way, wasn't what he meant to do. But damn it, she betrayed him again.

He heard her sniff as if she'd started crying and he felt like even more of an asshole. Which was insane because she started this. She broke a promise!

There was no way he could calm down, not with the rage boiling in his veins, but he remained quiet himself until he knew he wouldn't holler at her.

"I'm sorry," she whispered. "I had no intention of leaving."

"Why did you then?"

"My mom called. They're here at the hospital."

He should've known that would happen. Hell, he'd been the one to call them yesterday about Jason. He knew they were finding the first flight out of Italy. Of course they'd want Junelle at the hospital with them. What an idiot!

"That makes perfect sense why you left." He would give her that much. "But what doesn't make sense is why you didn't call me?" Why she broke her promise without even flinching?

"And if I had, what would you have said? Don't go?"

He gritted his teeth, hating how she might be right in that assessment. "Well, now we'll never know what I would've said."

"Abby and Bri came with me. They're still here. I told my parents everything. I won't be alone anywhere I go."

"You weren't alone when Jason was attacked either. Next time, it could be you instead of the other person."

She made a gurgled sound as if her tears had turned into sobs. More hatred at himself hit him. But the truth hurt. He wasn't going to hold back. Not when it came to her safety.

"I can't leave my parents. Not right now, Rider. Please understand."

Oh, he understood just fine. Nothing had changed between them. She still didn't trust him, not even enough to give him a courtesy call that she had to leave to be with her family.

"Sure. I understand."

He made eye contact with Stromberg, knowing he had to go. They had a killer to find.

"You're mad at me."

That was an understatement of the day.

"Go be with your parents."

"Rider..." His name came out in a strangled whisper, and it gutted him. "I'm sorry. Please don't be mad at me."

"I'll call you later." Or not. "That is, if you want me to."

Another sniffle echoed in his ear. "Yes, I want you to. I'll be with my parents all day. When you're done, come to the hospital."

That was the last thing he wanted to do. After five years of silence, her mom would grill him about his absence. Jason might know he and Junelle were once a thing—and approved of it—but what would her parents think?

"Rider? I need you. Please."

How in the hell could he ignore that kind of plea? Every fiber in his being wanted to.

"Yeah, I'll be there later. I gotta go."

Then he cut off the call before she could crush his heart even further.

He met Stromberg and Tate by the door.

"So, Cramer and Jackson are going to stick around and interview neighbors. See if anyone knows where we can find our mystery man who seems to have been pretending to be Roger. See if they heard anything or saw anything odd," Stromberg said. "We want to head back to the theater. That guy worked there for the past six months. Someone has to know where he'd hide."

He was fine with that.

"How's Junelle holding up?" Tate asked, as if he knew things were not well and wanted the full scoop.

"She left the apartment. Her mom called and she went to the hospital. Bri and Abby are still with her."

Stromberg winced and Tate looked like he wasn't surprised by that development.

"Abby will not hesitate to use her gun."

Rider was thankful for that, but it didn't make it any easier to swallow the fact Junelle broke her promise.

"Let's find this asshole." He walked out of the apartment

first. He was done talking about it. About everything. His goal today was to find this bastard, then get on with his life —without Junelle.

She'd made it clear where he stood in her life.

Outside of it.

They worked all day running down leads and interviewing people who knew the man they all thought was Roger Woodson. Between five detectives, they came up with nothing. While he wanted to push the autopsy on the man they thought was the real Roger Woodson to right this minute, that wouldn't be happening until tomorrow—at the earliest.

By seven o'clock, he was wiped and wanted nothing more than to go home and crash. Alone.

Instead, he found himself going to the hospital with Stromberg and Tate. They had to pick up the loves of their lives. He wished he was doing the same. But he figured Junelle would be going home with her parents. For the most part, it was for the best.

When he walked into the waiting area, before he could even get a word out, Janice, Jason's mother, was crushing him in a hug.

"When Jason recovers, you are going to get the biggest scolding a mother can give a child," she whispered in his ear. "I don't want to hear that crap you're not my son. You were in my home so often growing up, it was like I had two sons. When one stops communicating, well, that deserves a scolding."

He didn't know how much he needed a hug from her— his second mom—until the moment she had given him one. While he made no comment in return, he held on for dear life.

She was the first to pull away. "Now tell me what you know?"

"Not much. I suspect someone who works with Junelle, but we can't seem to find him. But I will. I won't let him hurt her. I'm sorry I—"

"Nope," she said, shaking her finger in his face like she used to when they came trailing in the house, dragging in mud when they played football in the rain. "You're not blaming yourself for Jason getting hurt. I know how you think. And it's not happening. I need you to do something for me."

He'd do anything for this woman. She'd been a rock, an immovable force when his mother died. Walking away from Jason—from all of them—five years ago had been one of the hardest things he had ever done.

"Anything. Just say it. It's done."

"My Junelle...my sweet little girl is barely hanging on. Oh, she puts on a brave front, but a mother knows. A mother always sees everything. I saw how you felt about her years ago. I saw your eyes dart to her the moment you walked into this room. I heard the love for her in your voice when you called with the most devastating news a mother can get. So I need you to do what you've always done for my Junelle. I need you to keep her together."

Of course she had to ask the one thing of him he couldn't deliver on. How could he do something like that when she continued to push him away? When she continued to show him that she didn't trust him. No faith he'd do anything and everything for her.

Funny how she asked the one thing he couldn't do, instead of the one thing he could. He could keep her safe. He wouldn't hesitate to agree to such a thing because seeing Junelle hurt was unimaginable. But this...

She reached up and placed a hand on his shoulder. "You've always had a way with her. Don't deny it. I knew before you even knew that you loved her as much as she loved you. I saw it all. Do your thing, whatever that is, and keep her from falling apart."

"I'll do my best."

"No, you'll do it. That's what I want to hear."

This woman gave no quarter. She demanded and he had to deliver.

"She doesn't want me to help her." She'd given that proof today when she broke her promise.

"Oh, Rider, I know you've been through a lot lately. She told us everything. I know this isn't easy on you either, but don't lie to yourself. Lying won't help. You want to pretend that's what you see. But it's because you're afraid. I get it. She told me what happened five years ago as well. We had nothing to do but chat today."

And no doubt, she gave Junelle no choice but to confess everything.

"So get over your insecurities or self-doubt or whatever you're doing to yourself, and do as I ask."

Leave it to Janice Swanson to cut to the heart of the matter without any bullshit. Maybe he *was* afraid of putting himself out there. But when Junelle kept giving him reasons to be leery, what was he supposed to do? Keep letting her eviscerate him?

"Okay."

She narrowed her eyes, assessing, as if she wanted him to comply with more than a simple word of agreement. "Good. Glad we had this chat. Jason's vitals were looking better earlier. The doctor didn't say he was getting better, but I know my son. He's getting better. His color looked much improved."

It was just like Janice to demand, even in a coma, that Jason listen to her and wake up.

"Now, take Junelle home and get some rest. You look tired. Make sure you eat a good meal."

Before she could insist on coming home with them, he decided it was time to take control of the situation.

"You have nothing to worry about, Janice. Not only did my mother teach me how to cook, you taught me as well. I think you and Mr. Swanson need to go home yourself. Jason wouldn't want you worrying like this all day long."

"You're so right, Rider." With that, all the life she'd displayed moments before deflated right out of her. Her husband, Justin, was by her side, pulling her into his arms.

He'd assumed Junelle would go home with her parents. Oh, how wrong he'd been to think that. He'd been wrong about so many things. How Jason would feel about him dating his sister. What her parents would think about it.

Maybe it was time he stopped assuming things.

Stromberg and Tate left with Abby and Bri. Jason's parents followed right away. That left him alone with Junelle.

"You ready to go?"

He decided not to address the fact she was going home with him. No doubt her mother told her what would happen when he arrived.

She walked side-by-side with him to the elevators, not saying a word.

The ride home was silent as well. He didn't know what to say, and she evidently didn't either. He made sure to keep his eyes and ears peeled the entire time, especially when they weren't in the vehicle. As soon as they were inside his apartment, he locked the door, feeling a hundred times better they were in the safety of his home.

"I need to take a shower." He felt disgusting after the day he had. Even though he hadn't touched the dead body, he always felt dirty being around one. "Then I'll make us something to eat."

Junelle still didn't say a word, but she made it known with a quick nod she heard him.

Janice asked him to do one thing, and he knew he was going to fail at it—miserably. Look at him now. He couldn't even get Junelle to speak to him.

14

HE WAS BACK to hating her. She could feel it. The moment they stepped inside his apartment, he ran away. Did he really have to shower? He didn't look dirty.

She threw her purse on the couch, glanced at the small mess on the counter from the brief cookie making, then froze.

Decisions were so hard to make. Even the tiny ones. Those especially could have the most devastating impact.

Yet, she'd come to a decision. In a split second. It would either improve the atmosphere she felt swallowing her whole or ruin her into a million pieces.

Abby said to make the first move.

Of course, Abby also said not to text him before they left and look where that got her. Back in the doghouse with him. She should've gone with her first instinct. Call him. Tell him her plans to leave. He was right. Now she'd never know what he might've told her.

While following Abby's advice the first time didn't pan out well, she was going to try it again. But this time the difference was her gut also said she needed to do this.

Pausing outside the bathroom door, she gathered all the courage she had left inside and then opened the door.

The curtain was pulled closed with the sound of water running. His clothes were in a rumpled pile on the floor. He must not have heard the door open because the curtain didn't move and the water didn't shut off. She closed the door with a quiet click, waiting a moment for him to react. Nothing still.

Time to forge on.

Her sweatshirt and shirt came off first, then her bra, joining his clothes on the floor. When the curtain still didn't push to the side, she removed her pants, underwear, socks, and shoes. Standing naked, hoping she wasn't making a colossal mistake, she dug deep for another ounce of bravery.

Now or never.

She pushed the curtain aside enough to crawl into the shower.

That noise finally had Rider turning around. She couldn't stop herself from staring in awe at the perfection before her. Strong, toned arms. A sculpted chest with abs on display that told her he worked out on a regular basis. A nice tiny trail of hair that led to his cock that was standing at attention, hard and ready to play. Powerful legs that told her he'd be able to hold her against the shower wall and pound into her without a problem. If he wanted her, that is. He hadn't said a word or moved closer yet.

She also saw the two scars from his knife wounds. They frightened her, so she didn't stare long. To think she could've lost him...

He blocked most of the spray of water, but the bit of heat that hit her didn't help to warm any part of her up. His unreadable expression chilled her to the bone.

She'd taken this chance and she had to follow through to the end. She took the first step toward him.

His scars drew her attention again, even though she didn't want them to. He flinched when she touched the scar near his shoulder. Then he inhaled sharply when her finger trailed down to the scar by his heart.

To think she could've lost him and she hadn't even known about it. She had no one to blame but herself.

When her hand kept moving down his chest and tickled over the bit of hair near his belly button, he grabbed her hand and stopped her.

"Do you want me to leave?" she whispered. He'd halted her movements, but he didn't say a word. She had no idea what he was thinking.

"If you touch me, I won't last a second." His voice was hoarse, telling her he was exerting a lot of energy to remain in control.

"So you want me to leave?" Because if she couldn't touch him, what else was there to do?

"I want to keep you safe."

She frowned, not understanding what he meant.

"I can't be distracted by anything." He looked pained, as if he was waging his own war in his mind. Like he wanted to push her away, yet his hand tightened around hers.

Her free hand cupped his cheek and she smiled at the way he leaned into it. He wasn't immune to her. She hadn't made the wrong decision joining him in the shower. He wanted to fight his attraction to her, but she wouldn't let him.

"Do I distract you?" she asked, moving closer, feeling more of the hot water hit her body.

"You know you do, June Bug. You always have." His gaze

was glued to her lips. The deep, intense stare gave her another shot of bravery.

She wove her hand up his bristled cheek and through his hair as she pressed her body against his. The sharp inhale was his only response. He didn't push her away. He didn't stop her from rubbing against him. Their hands didn't move either, trapped between their bodies.

"If I'm distracted, I can't protect you. We shouldn't do this. Last time I was distracted..."

Yes, she knew. He'd gotten hurt. Nearly died. Her family had been the reason for the distraction. He didn't want history to repeat itself.

Some of the courage she had walking in here melted away. Shouldn't do it? Or he didn't *want* to do it? There was a distinct difference, and she needed to know which one.

"It's my fault what happened between us. I ruined the best thing, and I don't know if I'll ever forgive myself for it. I understand if you want me to leave this room because of that. But that's the lone reason I will leave. I trust you with my life and I want this if you want it."

"I've never stopped wanting you," he whispered right before his lips captured hers.

The kiss was thorough and vigorous. All the emotions that had been simmering like a volcano about to burst between them erupted in the kiss. Their tongues dueling in a battle, neither wanting to concede. His hand let go of hers and he grabbed her around the waist, lifting her up to straddle his hips. The kiss didn't stop for one second.

Then she was against the wall, securely in his arms, and not one part of her felt unsafe. He'd die before he let anything happen to her, and she'd do the same. They couldn't be vulnerable if they were in it together.

The kiss turned bruising, before he stopped it abruptly, his chest heaving up and down. His brows puckered into a fierce frown and his gaze struggled with something she couldn't quite figure out. He still looked like he was in uncontrollable pain.

"I don't want to stop now. I need you so badly I feel like I could die if I don't have you." He winced as if the pain had intensified.

"Then why did you stop kissing me?"

"I don't have protection. Every part of me wants to ignore that and thrust deep inside of you."

She'd been with a few other guys in the past five years. She always used a condom in addition to being on the pill. Even back then, she and Rider had used a condom. Neither had been ready for children, and she couldn't say she was ready even now.

But the risk was worth it. To have him. To hold him. To never let go.

"Then let's ignore it. I'm on the pill."

He held her gaze for the longest time, his face twisting and turning in an aggrieved way as if he was still battling his own war.

He swallowed hard before adjusting her just right, and with one deep thrust he was embedded all the way inside her. His eyes closed as his forehead fell against hers.

"God, baby, give me a minute. You feel so damn good."

Her hands tightened against his back and her legs encircling his waist gripped him even harder.

His fingers dug into her ass as he hissed, "Don't move, June Bug."

She couldn't help but smile at the passion in his voice. This strong, stubborn man was at her mercy, and he knew it as much as she did.

After what felt like minutes, which was more like less than one, he lifted his head, his features taut and fierce.

"Hold on, baby. It's going to get rough."

Before she could respond to bring it on, his hips were moving. He thrusted in and out, loving her exquisitely against the shower wall. Her low moans of pleasure mingled with his growls as more than steam from the water filled the room.

His fingers clutched her ass, his thrusts powerful and strong. She felt the strength in him as his legs held her up as if she weighed nothing more than a feather. The entire time his eyes held hers, and she couldn't tear hers away from him. They were both mesmerized by the emotions flickering like a movie reel in fast forward motion.

"I can't hold back much longer," he groaned, his lips twisting in sweet, sweet agony.

"Let go, Rider. It's okay."

While the ecstasy was building inside her, she wasn't as close as him. She wouldn't deny him the pleasure to satisfy herself. He'd been a generous lover back then and she knew he hadn't changed. He'd make sure she felt good afterward.

"It's not okay," he half-shouted, half groaned. Then he tightened his grip on her, moving away from the wall. She didn't feel as secure, yet she felt the power in his embrace. He wouldn't let her fall. He stopped thrusting and stood there for a moment. "We come together or we don't come at all."

She giggled, then gasped when he lifted her and back down. A subtle rub, but enough to ignite her senses even more than before.

Over and over he did that. Small little lifts that created a beautiful friction between them. She felt the potency in every thrust. She felt the desire in every movement he made.

Her eyes closed when she knew she was nearing the pinnacle. "Don't stop, Rider. Please don't stop this time."

"Never, baby, never," he whispered close to her ear.

Then her back was against the wall again, his thrusts deep and slow until it hit her. An orgasm so electrifying her nails dug into his back and she screamed his name.

"Yes, June Bug. Squeeze me, baby!" Then he was tensing and growling his own pleasure, filling her up.

As the sensations pulsated through them, they stood silent, holding each other. He was the first to move, placing light kisses on her neck until he hit her mouth, depositing the sweetest kiss she'd ever been given.

"I still need to wash my hair."

She giggled again, smoothing her hand over his wet hair. "I insist I help then."

"I might've forgotten to wash my body too."

Her smile widened even more. "Is that right?"

He murmured yes as his lips drew up into a devilish smirk. "Every part of my body is still dirty."

"Then by all means, I need to help with that."

"Yes, you do."

Then no more words were spoken as his lips devoured hers until her body was lighting up for round two.

———

HIS EYES GRADUALLY OPENED, a bit of sunshine filtering through the window because he hadn't closed the curtains all the way last night. He hated getting woken up by the bright glare, but it didn't bother him today. Not with the beauty lying next to him.

Junelle was curled on her side, her head resting on her pillow, but her arm was flung across his chest. Right over his heart, blocking his view of the scar that always sent him into a tailspin when he stared at it too long.

He still couldn't believe she'd walked into the bathroom and made the first move. He wasn't sure why that surprised him. Maybe because he'd always been the aggressor in the relationship, especially five years ago. Hell, he wasn't complaining.

But he should be.

He couldn't afford to be distracted. One wrong move and she could be hurt. Or worse—die. He knew without even thinking about it, he'd die himself if something happened to her. She might've walked out of his life all those years ago, but his love for her had never stopped. That had always weighed on his mind more than he cared to admit. She'd dropped him like a hot potato without one chance to explain, yet his heart could never let go. He'd hated that about himself. That weakness he couldn't seem to control.

Though, now it made it easier to let her back into his life. To let the love he had for her run wild like it had a right to do so.

The shower last night had been the best damn shower he'd ever had. Their lovemaking didn't stop there. He had loved her body from head to toe several times throughout the night. Even now, knowing he had to get up and get to work, he wanted to love her again. Never leave the apartment for several weeks until he felt satisfied. Even then, he knew he wouldn't be satisfied.

But he had a killer to find. The sooner he did that, the sooner they could move forward with their lives.

Together.

He wasn't giving her up now. Not after last night.

Brushing his hand over her cheek, he smiled when her eyes opened into tiny slits.

"Wakey, wakey, sleepyhead."

Her dazzling emerald eyes closed. "No. Not yet."

The few times he'd spent the night five years ago, she hadn't been a fan of the morning. Apparently, that trait hadn't changed.

His hand wove down her side, tickling a few areas, before landing on her ass. He gripped her hard and pulled her into his arms until she was flush against him. She didn't open her eyes, but a low moan escaped.

Yes, his June Bug wasn't a fan of waking up, but she wouldn't resist his good morning to her.

His lips touched her mouth, before making a tender path across her chin and to her neck, nibbling in spots. Her breathing increased and her hips moved, trying to get closer. One hand stayed glued to her ass while his other hand glided to the front of her body and down below where he found her wet and ready for him. His fingers rubbed a delicate pattern, his lips devouring every spot he could find while her sweet moans filled the room.

"Come for me, baby," he whispered in her ear, then nibbled it. His fingers increased the pressure, one slipping inside her.

It didn't take too much longer after that for her to scream his name, trembling in his arms. God, he'd never get tired of hearing his name come out of her mouth like that.

He rolled her onto her back, and with one swift move, he was deep inside her. As much as he wanted to remain still for a moment and savor how wonderful it felt, he couldn't. His need for her was too great.

His thrusts were hard and deep. Over and over as the pleasure built inside of him. Her eyes opened wide as her legs wrapped around his waist. Yes. He wanted to see her bright, decadent eyes looking at him. The sultry smile that lit up her face urged him on even more. Even harder. Even deeper. Her back arched at the penetration, her sweet moans filling the room.

"I want you to come again. With me this time," he said, unwrapping her legs and lifting them to his shoulders to get even deeper. "I won't come until you do."

Then his fingers found the spot he knew she loved, working their magic as he thrusted with vigor.

She cried out first, the wondrous sound filling up his soul that had been so broken for the longest time. He joined her in bliss, tensing and growling her name as he held her close, refusing to pull out when he should've.

His entire body relaxed, losing its energy. He let her legs go and curled her into his body, still deep inside her.

"I don't want to leave this bed," he whispered, holding her tight. Though she didn't answer with words, the fierce grip she had on him was answer enough. She didn't want to leave either.

Then he lifted his head, and despite not wanting to, his lips twisted into a frown. "But we have to get ready."

"We do." Two soft spoken words, but they were enough to give him the strength to pull out, roll to a seated position, and climb out of bed. He wished she wouldn't have agreed so easily with him.

"I'm going to skip a shower. I'll be quick in the bathroom and then you can have it."

"I'll skip one too."

They were on the same wavelength then. Another shower, by either of them, would result in more lovemaking. That wasn't something they could afford to do. Not right now, anyway. Playtime was over. It was time to catch a killer.

He brushed his teeth, combed and styled his hair as best as he could, and finished with a quick trim to his beard. He dressed while she used the bathroom. They both convened in the kitchen at the same time.

"I can make some eggs and toast if you want some." He didn't eat much in the mornings, but he'd make sure she was satisfied before they left.

"Toast is fine. Or a bagel if you have any."

He didn't, but the next grocery run he'd make sure to add it to his list. "Only toast, sorry."

She gave him a quick peck on the cheek before grabbing the bread from the cupboard. "It's okay. I'd love coffee though. Please tell me you have that at least."

"Definitely."

He started preparing the coffee while she made her toast. They didn't even venture to the kitchen once when they got home last night, so she also cleaned up the mess she and the other two ladies made before they left.

"What were you three making?"

"Cookies," she replied as she put a bag of flour and sugar in his cupboard. Chocolate chips followed it.

He knew he didn't have the full ingredients for cookies, so Abby or Bri brought it over. As much as it bugged the hell out of him they let Junelle leave yesterday, risking her safety, he appreciated the forethought on trying to keep her busy. If only they would've stayed. He wouldn't have worried about her as much *and* he could be munching on a delicious treat for breakfast.

"So about today."

She turned around from the fridge with the butter in her hand, looking weary. "Yes?"

They made serious ground yesterday in their relationship, even if it had been rocky a few times. He didn't want to send them backward. Not even an inch. So making demands wouldn't get him closer to her but farther away.

"I'm dropping you off at the hospital? Or Abby and Bri are hanging out with you here?"

The worry slid away from her features as a bright smile lit up her lips. "I'd like to be with my parents today. I'm sure they're going back, if not already there." She set the butter on the counter and wound her arms around him. "Thank you for giving me a choice."

If he had his way, he'd lock her far, far away from everyone, where no one would be able to find her. Since he knew that was unreasonable and a ridiculous thing to even think, he went with the smarter option. Giving her what she wanted.

"I'm not going to stop you from doing anything. I want you to be safe. If anything happened to you..." He pressed his lips together, stopping himself from blurting out something he couldn't take back. She didn't need to know how terrified he was of losing her. Especially now that he had her back in his life.

"Yeah, well, the same goes for you. If anything happened to you..." Then her words trailed off and she finished her sentence with a tender kiss.

Then they went back to breakfast. Her eating her toast and sipping on coffee while he gulped his and poured another cup.

"Call your parents before we leave. I'm not leaving you alone until they get there."

"I will." She picked up her phone, her fingers tapping away before setting it back down. "Just texted my mom." It pinged right away. "They're on their way to the hospital now."

"Good." He'd meet up with Stromberg and Tate at the precinct after dropping her off. Now to the part he wanted to avoid forever. "I have a question. Or two."

The weariness was back on her face and he hated it. "Okay."

"How well do you know Roger Woodson? He's a security guard at the theater where you work."

Or so the man had claimed. Not that he wanted to confess that.

She shrugged. "I don't recognize the name. I mean, I don't know everyone in the building."

He grabbed his phone and showed her the driver's license photo of the real Roger Woodson.

"I've never seen him before. He works at the theater?"

Damn it. No, he didn't. Now he had to confess everything. It had been inevitable. He found a picture of the imposter, a photo they'd gotten from the theater. The man had worn a security badge with his photo on it. It still blew Rider's mind that this man had never feared being discovered about his duplicity.

A slight shiver hit her body as she stared at the face. Her brows puckered, as if trying to remember interacting with him.

"I didn't know his name, but I've seen him around the theater."

While he'd hoped she wouldn't have recognized him, he wasn't surprised.

"And," he prompted when she appeared to zone out.

"And I try to keep my distance. He's always given me a weird feeling. I mean, he's never been mean or anything, but he's...weird."

He was also a killer. Though he kept that to himself.

"Has he ever asked you out?"

Junelle set her coffee down, her hand shaking as she let the mug go. "I gave you that list already. Do you think he's the one who sent me all those letters? That he killed Molly?"

Or not. He couldn't keep his suspicions to himself, not if he wanted her to stay safe.

"I do. And I also think he killed Paul."

She wrapped her arms around herself, shaking her head. "But why?"

He set his own mug down and pulled her into his arms. "I have no idea, sweetheart. I wish I did, but I don't. But I think it's all related and he's at the center of it. I don't even know where to start to explain. We found a dead body in Roger Woodson's apartment yesterday. Except the body we found *is* Roger Woodson, and it's the man I showed you the first picture of. The man you know, the second photo, he's been impersonating the real Woodson. He was the one driving the car in your neighborhood. He's the one who works at the theater. No doubt, he's the one who killed Paul. It's messed up, but I'm going to connect all the dots and get this bastard."

"That's horrible. I don't understand." She uttered a vicious curse before burying her head in his chest. "I barely said a word to the man. Why would he write such things to me?"

His arms tightened around her. "Probably because you didn't say much to him. He took offense to it or something. Who knows. He's twisted in the head. But I won't let him hurt you, and he will pay for hurting Jason. I promise you that."

Her head lifted. "I know you will. We should go so this can be all over with. I want to go back to normal."

So did he.

Except what was normal?

Because she better have meant a normal that now included him. He wouldn't except anything less.

15

RIDER TRIED to make the conversation quick with Junelle's parents, but Janice was never one to rush. She did things on her own time and expected everyone to do as she wished. Since he hadn't seen her in so long, he let her, even if he had a million things to do today.

Junelle saved him from inquisition—Janice wanting to know every aspect of the case—and pushed him out of the waiting area.

While he appreciated her help in escaping, he didn't get a goodbye kiss either. The entire drive to the precinct, he couldn't determine if that had been intentional or not. She either forgot and wanted to help him leave. Or she didn't kiss him because she didn't want her parents to find out.

The simple forgotten gesture bothered him more than he cared to admit.

Tate and Stromberg were already at work when he arrived later than he had intended. He'd texted them Junelle's plans earlier so Abby and Bri didn't show up at his place. He stood for a moment by his desk before sitting down. Damn. He had good friends. They were looking out for someone they didn't even know. All that mattered was she mattered to him.

What had he been doing?

Acting like a colossal ass. To everyone. That had to stop now.

He turned away from his desk and headed toward Stromberg and Tate. They both looked up at him. Hell, he should've stopped at their desk when he arrived. Instead, he did his usual thing. Walked past them without a word hello or even a glance in their direction. His assholish behavior would stop right now. No more.

At least, with these two. They deserved that respect and so much more for their help with keeping Junelle safe.

"I never said thank you to either of you. Or Abby or Bri. They deserve so many thanks for being there for Junelle, someone they don't even know."

Tate smirked, leaning back in his chair. "Gosh, did that hurt you to say? And with a smile."

He hadn't been focusing on his expression, but he made sure to wipe it clear after that remark.

"Ignore him. He's been pissy since he arrived," Stromberg said, waving a frivolous hand toward Tate. "You don't have to thank us. That's what friends are for."

He nodded. No way in hell he'd voice out loud any more gratitude if that was how Tate was going to respond.

"How is Jason?" Stromberg asked.

"Nothing new to report." Yet. Hopefully soon he'd have good news. He couldn't determine if no new changes were a good thing. Sure, not getting bad news was wonderful. But he figured some good news would have at least popped up. Why wasn't he waking up? Why hadn't they moved him from the ICU yet? Brain activity was good, which was no surprise there. He hadn't suffered a head injury. He'd lost a lot of blood, but he had a transfusion, with no problems there. His blood pressure was doing well. No hiccups with his heartbeat.

But Jason had spent too many hours in surgery as the doctors tried to repair a lot of internal bleeding. Hell, he'd been stabbed five times. That was the problem. He'd suffered such a brutal attack, his body was struggling to heal.

Only time would tell.

And time wasn't something Rider was good at. He liked results. Without delay.

"Well, we have some interesting news for you," Tate said, sitting back up straight. "Autopsy was performed on the dead man we found in Woodson's apartment. Cause of death was sharp force trauma, most likely a knife of some kind was used. No surprise there since that's how Paul was murdered, as well as Molly. Jason was also attacked by a knife. I would venture a guess that it's been the same knife used in all cases."

Stromberg jerked his head in agreement. He couldn't find fault in that logic either.

Tate continued, "The coroner was able to get fingerprints from the body to help with identification. Did you know when a body is frozen and then unthawed it deteriorates very rapidly?"

He didn't know that, and at the moment didn't care because the coroner had gotten the necessary information to determine the cause of death and get fingerprints. Confirming the identity of the victim was crucial.

When he didn't respond, Tate grinned. "You're going to love this."

He very much doubted he would love whatever Tate was

about to say. Because he wasn't loving anything about this case.

"The body has been identified as Roger Woodson."

Rider stared at him. They all thought that would be the outcome, but it still came as a surprise and it shouldn't have.

"Damn it. Having confirmation really doesn't help us. I want to know who the other guy is!"

Tate's grin didn't disappear, and Rider wanted to smack the look right off his face. What was there to smile about? Asshole.

Maybe he muttered the explicit word under his breath instead of merely thinking it, or maybe Tate finally got his head out of his ass, but he dropped the cocky smile.

"The coroner couldn't give a time of death. Not even an estimate because the body was frozen rock solid. And considering Roger—or the person we thought was Roger—was seen only a day ago, it couldn't have been the man in the freezer who stabbed Jason. The body in the freezer did not kill anyone. Hasn't in some time if I had to guess."

"I don't get it. I want to find this bastard. None of that information helps us do that."

"It's messed up, man," Stromberg said. "We know Roger signed his lease six months ago. Mr. Delgati told us yesterday he doesn't remember which man signed the lease."

"That guy probably doesn't want to be liable for anything," Tate added.

Stromberg continued. "We also know the mystery man worked at the theater for the past six months. Same as the lease." Stromberg's fingers tapped hard on his keyboard, pulling up a photo on his computer.

Rider turned his attention to it. The man who worked at the theater, courtesy of the security department requiring photos. Then Stromberg did a few more taps on the keyboard. A different photo popped up. Right next to the other one. The driver's license of the real Roger Woodson.

Different guy. But not by much. Same dirty blonde hair. Same eye color. Bone structure kind of the same. They couldn't pass as twins, but they were similar looking.

"Mystery man," Stromberg said, pointing at the photo on the right. Then he gestured at the photo to the left. "The man found in the freezer and identified as Roger Woodson. I'm not sure how the mystery man was hired at the theater for a security position when these photos do not match. Serious screw-up there. Talk about shit security if they don't even do a background check on potential employees."

Great point by Stromberg. Again, that didn't help solve their dilemma. How did they find the mystery man? That's what he needed!

They weren't just looking for a disgruntled employee attacking their co-workers. They were looking for a damn serial killer who took on the identity of his victims. Or at least some of them.

"We're looking for a damn ghost," Rider said through gritted teeth, then swore up a storm.

"Unfortunately," Tate replied, more subdued than minutes before. "No viable prints were found at Junelle's. No good prints were found at Paul's either. We need to wait for forensics to do their job from all the prints they collected yesterday from Woodson's apartment. Hopefully, we'll get a hit from there. They're still working on her damn letters. Slow as molasses."

Not surprising. The lab was always backed up.

"Look, we know what car he's driving, assuming he still has Woodson's vehicle. And we know what he looks like. That's something," Stromberg added.

But it wasn't enough. Rider wanted more than that. He wanted a damn name! A real one.

"The cat." Rider snapped his fingers. "Is it Woodson's cat? Because it wasn't on the lease, which makes me think this killer brought it with him."

Tate's brows drew low as he crossed his arms. "A killer who brutally murders a dog, but owns a cat. That's messed up."

The entire case was messed up.

"Let's call animal control and see if the cat has a microchip." Rider would take care of it himself. "I want this asshole's name. Then I want him found now."

One might be easier than the other. He hoped like hell he got some sort of lead to follow because Junelle's life depended upon it.

───────

THE DAY DRAGGED ON. Time seemed to slow down to a stop as she waited with her parents in the ICU waiting area. They did take turns checking on Jason, sitting with him for short periods of time. Junelle tried to keep her visits brief because the beeping of the monitors and seeing him look so deathly pale was too much. If she lost her brother...

Those weren't thoughts she wanted to have, yet that's all she had for the majority of the day. It didn't help being in the hospital either, keeping those thoughts at bay.

Her mother liked to keep conversation going. Junelle didn't mind engaging with her, but when it became too much at times, she retreated to another corner in the room. Her mother never argued, which she appreciated.

She texted with her friends. Co-workers checked in with her. She got updates about Paul's memorial service coming up and the gossip going around that Roger Woodson had something to do with it.

While she wanted to know everything going on, those conversations were hard as well. Because she was smack dab in the middle of it all, and it was too much.

So damn much.

As selfish as it felt, she wanted to leave and go back to Rider's. Of course, not alone. She wanted Rider to join her. Cuddle under the blankets and not leave for weeks. The real world didn't work like that and she knew even if it did, she couldn't go through with it. Her brother needed her, and Rider had to find the killer.

Because she couldn't stop herself, she texted Rider several times throughout the day. Last night had been everything and more. Something she thought she'd never get back again. All it took was the guts to put herself out there.

But would it last?

Would time apart remind him of all the ways she'd broken his trust—his heart?

So maintaining some sort of connection felt like a do-or-die situation. He always responded without making her wait long. While she didn't want to read too much into that, she appreciated that it didn't take him forever to reply. She hoped he felt the exact same way as her. Completely and utterly in love.

Maybe that was too much wishful thinking. But she'd do it anyway because she had nothing but time on her hands.

Lunchtime rolled around. They ventured to the cafeteria where they had half-decent food. They chatted as if they weren't in a hospital worried about someone they cared about. Sometimes you had to pretend everything was good or your entire world would fall apart.

She asked her parents questions about Italy and everything they had seen. Of course, her mom went into great detail, describing things so vividly, she felt like she'd gone on the vacation herself. It was too bad it had been cut short. Her parents had saved up for the longest time to take the trip. Ripped away with ease by one disturbed man.

Again, no matter how hard she tried, her mind always ventured into despair. Pulling herself out of it took a lot of effort, and her mom helped the rest of the way. Her upbeat, continuous monologue gave a person no choice.

After lunch, they went back to the waiting area and repeated the same routine as before. While she didn't want to eat hospital food again, no doubt they would. She didn't foresee Rider coming to the hospital until much later.

If luck was on their side, he and his co-workers would find the person responsible for all of this.

Roger Woodson. Or the man pretending to be him.

The name didn't give her the heebie-jeebies. It was just a name.

But when she conjured his face in her mind, that produced a round of shivers so severe, she couldn't stop them for several minutes. *That* was also a horrible thing that happened on repeat as much as the dire thoughts that entered.

She rarely spoke to the man at the theater. The few times she did, it had been a simple hello or goodbye. There wasn't anything particular that he had done to give her bad vibes. He simply had. If someone would ask her to explain why, she wasn't sure she'd be able to give a good enough reason. All she knew was that there had always been something in his eyes that frightened her. A glint of something... evil? Danger? Whatever it was, alarm bells had always gone off and she had kept her interactions short, and most of the time, non-existent.

Maybe that's what had been her downfall. Not giving him the attention he thought he deserved.

But how was she to know he'd turn out to be a psychotic killer?

No doubt, that wouldn't have stopped him from latching on to her anyway. He might've taken one look at her and decided in his mind she would be his next target.

"Hey, what's the matter?" her mom asked, touching her arm.

She blinked several times, trying to get her bearings back. She'd fallen into another rabbit hole of misery. Her mom had been speaking about something, but she wouldn't be able to repeat any of it back if asked.

The last thing she intended to do was tell her mom where her thoughts had taken her.

"Just chilly. It's cold in here." A simple explanation for the tremble that touched her. Not that it was the real reason for it.

"It's always cold in hospitals. I can have your father go home and get you a sweater."

"No, Mom, it's okay, but I appreciate it. I think I'll go check on Jason again. It is a bit warmer in his room."

That wasn't a lie, but it didn't matter. She hadn't been cold to begin with, so whether his room was warmer or not had no bearing on anything. Her mother didn't need to know any of that though.

"He'll like that. Talk to him for a bit. They won't kick you out."

That was the polite way for her mom to tell her to visit longer than she usually did. This time she would try harder.

Because she was right. Jason would like it. If he could hear her, that is. The more they tried to connect with him, the more chance he'd pull through all of this. She had to believe that.

She hugged her mom before leaving the room and made her way to Jason's side. The lights were off, but the curtains were half open, letting in some light. But the semi-darkness made the room feel heavier, more subdued. She didn't turn on the lights though.

The chair made a loud scraping sound as she scooted it closer to his bed. Then she sat down, facing the door. She'd be able to see anyone who walked in.

His hand was warm, yet his skin was pale. She lifted it and clung to it, squeezing extra hard. No response from him, yet she hadn't expected one.

"Umm....so I shouldn't have this kind of conversation with you, but you'd jump with joy if you could right now." She bit her lip, wondering why she decided to go right to this detail going on in her life. "I slept with Rider last night. I made the first move. Can you believe it? I can't. You wouldn't either, I bet."

She wasn't shy when it came to men, but reserved. Leery. One wrong moment had done that to her. That moment had turned out to be something it wasn't. Joke was on her.

Not to mention, she had given her heart to Rider. Putting it back together and giving it to someone else had never been her intention. Not when it had hurt so much to lose him. Why go through something so devastating again? Purposely put herself in that position?

But last night she had. She'd put her heart on the line, and he hadn't crushed it. He'd embraced it—her.

"It didn't feel like it felt five years ago. It felt...I don't know...like more. More powerful. More of something that terrifies me. If I lose him again, I don't know how I'd survive it a second time." She lifted Jason's hand, pulling it to her chest. "If I lose you...well, I can't. So please get better and wake up. I need you in my corner. I need you pushing us together. I don't know how Rider feels or what he's thinking, and well, I'm giving you credit for getting us this far. So I need you for the rest of it."

Of course he didn't answer. She knew he wouldn't, yet the silence gutted her. It shoved home the reminder he was damn near knocking on heaven's door when he didn't respond. Didn't twitch in the slightest. Hell, watching his chest move, she could barely see him breathing. But all the monitors hooked up to him displayed everything was good.

She had to maintain that kind of hope. Everything would be good. Jason would pull through and tell her all would be well.

"I love you, Jason."

The door opened.

She looked up to see a doctor walk in. Shadows covered his face until he neared the bed.

The man had dirty-blonde hair with a brown mustache. He smiled at her but had his attention on Jason.

"How is he doing?"

Odd. That was the question she wanted to ask him. He was the doctor. He'd know more than her.

"Same as always." She didn't know how to answer.

The doctor nodded. Then produced a vile and a needle. He inserted the needle into the vial, filling it up.

"What's that for?"

"To help him. I promise."

Then he picked up the IV line, removed the needle portion off the syringe, and attached it to the IV.

He looked up at her.

The moment his gaze met hers, she froze. The grip she had on Jason's hand intensified.

"Aww, so do you know who I am." Roger Woodson smiled. A wicked, horrible smile that filled her veins with ice. "If you scream or even make a tiny sound, I will inject this."

Her eyes widened, but she dipped her head once that she understood. That was the most she could do.

"Take your purse off and set it on the windowsill. Far enough away from you. Show me your phone so I know it's in there and not on your person."

With deep reluctance, she let go of Jason's hand and removed the strap of her purse from across her body. She produced her phone, showing it to him, then let it drop back into the bag. She tossed the entire thing behind her, letting it drop to the windowsill with a loud thump.

His expression morphed from humorous to deadly in an instant. His finger twitched. "I said to not make even a tiny sound. Why do you disrespect me so much?"

"I'm sorry."

And, oh, god she was so very sorry. Whatever was in that syringe, she knew it would kill Jason. It would finish the job the man had originally tried to do.

"Now walk around to this side of the bed."

What did he plan to do?

Did it even matter? While he had his finger on the trigger button to Jason's death, she had to comply. So she did. Stopping a few feet from him.

"Closer."

Her steps faltered, her entire body trembling as she moved a foot away from him. "Please don't hurt my brother."

"He's in pain, Junelle. I'm helping him." He pushed down on the syringe.

Before she could stop him, or even scream, he'd pressed down on the device, releasing all the liquid, snatched the syringe out, and then grabbed her roughly by the arm. She felt the knife, not seeing it once.

"Now we're going to walk out of here like nothing is wrong. Because if you make a commotion, you're going to regret it. And maybe they'll be able to save Jason if you don't make a ruckus. But if you do, all their attention will be on you, not him. Then you'll be the cause of his death. Not me."

With that, he pulled her from the room.

She didn't fight back at all.

16

SOMETIMES, working a case and finding the answers but being unable to do anything about it was the worst part of the job.

They'd made great headway on putting some of the puzzle pieces together.

After calling animal control, Rider wasn't surprised the cat hadn't been Roger Woodson's. The real Roger had signed a lease for the apartment, which was why the file had no record of the cat. So their mystery man had brought the cat with. Or The Ghost as Stromberg had dubbed him. Something that irritated Tate to no end when Stromberg gave killers a nickname. It didn't bug Rider at all. It helped him differentiate their mystery man with Roger Woodson when their lives were so intertwined.

They were able to confirm the lease was the real Roger because his signature didn't match with the signature on the paperwork with the theater. Six months ago, Roger started a year lease. One week later, The Ghost got a job at the theater. So they could only conclude, The Ghost had murdered Roger, stuffed his body in a freezer, and taken control of his identity within one week. Because Roger hadn't lived long in the apartment building, The Ghost had done it without any issues.

When shown a picture of Roger and The Ghost, all the residents on his floor had picked out The Ghost as the man who lived there. None of them could recall seeing Roger. The super hadn't been able to remember who he dealt with when the lease was signed. It didn't matter. They had a rough timeline of Roger's murder.

The cat had a microchip. That information sent them down a whole new mystery. Charles, the cat, had been registered to Stan Barkley, who lived in Ohio. After making a few phone calls, they found out that Mr. Barkley had been found murdered about six and a half months ago—presumably by The Ghost. So he killed Mr. Barkley, stole the cat—reason unknown—moved to New York City, found another victim, and took over his identity.

When Rider spoke to the detective on Mr. Barkley's case, he'd been a loner, no family and very limited amount of friends. He'd move into his rental and had been found coincidently in a freezer as well, eight months later. Rider knew once they did a full deep dive into the real Roger's life prior to moving into that apartment, they'd find he had been a loner too.

Rider assumed this was The Ghost's MO. Find someone with no ties with anyone, recently moved, kill them, assume their identity, live life until he decides it's time to move on. The difference with Mr. Barkley's case and Roger's was while people had been hurt and killed where The Ghost worked at the theater, nothing of that nature happened with Mr. Barkley. He'd gotten a job at a manufacturing warehouse, did a good job but kept to himself. They didn't have a reason why he decided to up and move. No other murders in the area could be tied to him. But Rider didn't doubt that The Ghost murdered more than just Mr. Barkley when he lived in Ohio.

Once they found this man, he knew they'd learn of more identities he'd stolen, more places he'd killed people.

No useful evidence had been found in Mr. Barkley's residence. No fingerprints that didn't match the real Mr. Barkley. No DNA. Nothing to help them determine The Ghost's real identity.

When forensics eventually got back to them about Roger's apartment, he figured they'd get the same answer. Nothing. Nada. Zilch.

So while they had started a history of The Ghost and where he'd come from, they weren't any closer in identifying him or gaining any clues of where to find him. Rider liked to hope the man decided it was best to move on and start a new life in a new place. But he knew that wasn't the case.

He had unfinished business.

Junelle.

As soon as he wrapped that up, he'd disappear once again. Of course, Rider would never let that happen. Junelle wasn't getting hurt on his watch.

His phone rang, startling him, he'd been so lost in his thoughts. Janice. Why was she calling him and not Junelle?

"Hey, is everything okay?" He heard loud beeping in the background, voices raised as if a huge commotion was going on.

"It's Jason! He's...I don't know. His heart stopped." Her voice was low and calm, but he heard the terror. Janice knew how to remain in control, but a person could only maintain that to a certain point. "I can't find Junelle. She was sitting with him, but she's not here."

He stood up so fast, his chair flew behind him and

toppled to the floor. She would've never left her brother alone. Not if she was sitting with him and he'd gone into a medical emergency.

"I'm on my way. I'll call hospital security. Don't worry about her. I'll find her."

He ended the call before Janice could argue or even say one word. He couldn't afford to get into a long conversation with her.

"Let's go!" he yelled at Stromberg and Tate as he rushed past their desks. He didn't stop to see if they followed. Though he could hear the hurried footsteps behind him.

He called the hospital security, giving them Junelle's description along with The Ghost's. He wanted a full-on lockdown of the hospital. The person he spoke to refused such a request. So he demanded his supervisor. That yielded the same results. They wouldn't put the hospital on a lockdown.

"At least search the damn hospital for her! If something happens to her, I'll hold you personally responsible."

Then he hung up, shoving his phone in his pocket, and yanked open his car door. Stromberg got into the front passenger seat while Tate jumped into the back.

"What happened?" Stromberg asked, holding onto the dashboard as he peeled out of the parking lot.

"Jason took a turn for the worse. His mom said his heart stopped. Junelle was sitting with him, but she's not in the area. She would've never left him alone."

Stromberg swore under his breath while Tate said nothing.

Silence filled the car.

Fine by him. He didn't need empty reassurances or hopeful speeches all would be well. Because they didn't know that. They couldn't know that.

A ring tore through the quiet.

"Abby, now's not a good time—" Tate started, then inhaled sharply. A slew of curse words rushed out. "Hold on, let me put you on speaker. I'm with Rider and Stromberg. Go ahead."

"We're at the hospital. Junelle is with a man that we don't recognize and she looks terrified."

Rider tensed, his hands tightening on the wheel. For a split second he regretted driving. His mind wanted to unlatch from itself, yet he remained in control as he took a sharp right. "Describe him."

Abby did so, and Rider wanted to punch something. That matched The Ghost to a T. Except for the mustache. He must've decided he needed a disguise if he was going to get close to Junelle.

"Shit, they went into the elevator. We're too far away to get on with them," Abby said, then continued. "Bri, let's take the stairwell. I imagine they're heading for the first floor."

"Abby, be careful," Tate said.

"You too, Briella!" Stromberg added.

"Better yet. Stop following him."

Rider couldn't believe Tate even said that. "Don't you dare stop following him!" He wanted to turn around and glare, spit at him, anything, for saying such a thing.

A deadly silence filled the air.

"I'm sorry, Rider. I don't want to see Junelle get hurt, but I also don't want Abby hurt either. What happens if he notices them and hurts Junelle."

"Tate, stop talking. You're making it worse," Abby's voice filtered in. "I got...this. We...got this." Her breathing was heavy and her sentences were broken up. No doubt from running down several flights of stairs. "This is not...my first time spying...on someone. He won't see us."

Tate let loose a merciful laugh. "Umm...the first time didn't go so well, or don't you remember?"

She returned her own laugh. "Oh no, the spying part went marvelous." More heavy breathing filled the air. "He never saw me once. It was the visit...that was my undoing. So stop it, Tate."

Rider wanted to know more of the story, but not right now. His focus had to be on Junelle. Getting her out of this mess unharmed.

"Shit. The elevator didn't stop on the first floor."

Or they didn't run fast enough.

There was another thirty seconds of silence but with heavy breathing before Abby spoke again, this time in a whisper. "He's heading toward the parking garage. Damn it. We didn't drive here. We don't have a vehicle to follow him."

"We're five minutes away." Rider pushed harder on the gas, beeping for people to get out of the way since they weren't responding fast enough to the sirens he'd lit up.

While they weren't five minutes away, he'd make damn sure he turned it into that. There was no other option. He had to get there. Now!

"Okay, no, he's not getting in a car. He appears to be going through the parking garage. We're on the street now. He's going for the subway. I think."

"Abby, I need to know. Not what you think," Rider snapped.

"Hey, watch your tone," Tate warned.

Whatever. He wasn't going to worry about being pleasant when the woman he loved was in the clutches of a madman.

"Shit. He's going down another street. Hold on."

The few short seconds of silence tore at his heart and

ripped his gut apart. He needed to know what the hell was going on. What she was seeing.

"Oh no. Damn it."

"What?" He was afraid to ask. "What is it?"

Abby took a large inhale before speaking. "We can't see them anymore. I waited too long to peek around the corner when they turned the corner and I don't know where they went."

His worst nightmare had come true. His best friend was dead, and the love of his life was about to be next.

JUNELLE TRIED to not make it easy for this man to drag her away from the hospital, but every time she even flinched in the wrong direction, he dug the knife in her side. She knew it had broken skin. She felt blood trickling down. If he shoved it any harder, it would start gushing and she didn't need that.

The only blessing she had right now was she wasn't alone. She'd seen Abby and Bri as he forced her out of the ICU area. She and Abby had made very brief eye contact. She didn't stare too long at them because she didn't want to make him aware someone knew what was going on. Not turning around to see if they were following had been difficult.

They'd ducked down another street devoid of any other person and at the second set of doors to the left, they'd entered the building. Now, as he pulled her along the corridor, she strained her ears to hear the opening and closing of the door they'd entered. So far nothing.

But they had to still be following her. Abby and Bri would stop at nothing to stay on her tail. She knew it! Hell,

Abby carried a gun around with her. She wouldn't do that if she wasn't prepared to use it.

They walked down the hallway, making a left, then a right, then another left before he opened a door and shoved her inside. She fell hard to the ground, her right elbow smacking into the floor with a painful bang. Pain jolted up her arm, making her wince.

Light filled the room.

She wanted to glance around to see where she was, but she couldn't tear her gaze off him. The last thing she could afford was to underestimate him.

He flung off the doctor's white lab coat, tossing it to the floor. Then he tore off the fake mustache. He hadn't needed to wear that to throw her off who he was. His eyes had told her the moment they made contact. The knife was hanging by his side. Though she couldn't see any blood dripping from it, she knew it had torn skin. She felt the wound on her side. It stung, but it wasn't as bad as the pain pulsating in her elbow.

Even though she wanted to wrap her arm close to her chest, as if that would relieve the pain, she kept it by her side, not wanting to give any hint that he'd hurt her.

He stepped inside the room and shut the door, flipping the lock.

"Why are you doing this?" She couldn't believe she found the strength to speak. But she wanted answers.

Plus, she needed to keep him distracted until help arrived. And help would arrive. She had to keep the faith it would.

Abby and Bri followed her! Rider would be right behind them. She knew it. She had to hold on to that hope.

"The better question is why do people disrespect me so? I do so much for everyone, and yet, I get no respect."

The man was delusional. What had he ever done for her other than terrify her? Send her threatening and disturbing letters?

"I'm respecting you. I listened and followed directions and you still hurt my brother. Why?"

What had she done to this man to deserve this kind of treatment?

"I relieved him from his pain. You should be thanking me."

She'd let him kill her before she ever uttered such a thing.

"What did you inject him with?"

He smirked. "A lovely concoction that won't show up on any toxicology report. It'll look like his heart stopped and he'll have a painless death. Again, you're welcome."

They might believe he had nothing to do with it. Jason was fighting for his life from the stabbing. It wouldn't be unreasonable for him to go into cardiac arrest.

But her death? He'd never be able to hide anything from that.

Did it even matter? He'd get away with it. Just like he did with Jason. She didn't even fight back. She could've. She could've saved her brother's life. Instead, she willingly let this monster kill him.

"What are you going to do with me?"

Was this where he raped her? Violated her in every way he'd detailed in those letters he sent her?

They'd horrified her reading them. She couldn't even imagine what it would feel like to experience them.

She figured she was about to find out.

He took a step forward.

She scrambled back, crying out in pain when the ache in her elbow flared up at the movement.

That induced the vicious smile he wore to increase as he kept advancing. She had nowhere to go when she backed up against what she assumed was a desk. A metal desk if the clanging noise that echoed in the room was any indication. A brief glance at the walls showed filing cabinets lining them. She was in an office of sorts.

He crouched down, shoving the knife against her throat, preventing her from trying to escape.

"I'm going to make you pay for every ounce of disrespect you treated me with. Hands out in front of you." He pressed the knife deeper when she didn't comply.

She felt blood trickle down her throat. There was no running from any of this. She brought her hands up.

"Good girl. Don't move. Not even an inch."

She swallowed hard, fear crawling all over her skin. He stood up, went to the lab coat, and dug out a roll of duct tape. Then he was back by her side. Once again, she let him control her, sitting there as he wrapped her wrists together so tightly they ached. He used so much of the duct tape, it'd be impossible to break through it with the meager strength she had.

He stood up, dragging her by her wrists to stand as well. Everything about it hurt, making her cry out. She hated the show of weakness. All it did was make him smile.

He pushed her toward the left side of the room where an old radiator heater sat against the wall. He wasn't gentle as he shoved her to the ground.

"Hands up."

She wanted to fight back. To show him that she wasn't afraid.

Except he put the knife to her throat and all it did was produce tears, more blood to trickle down, and her hands to raise toward him.

"That's what I thought."

He set the knife down away from her, then proceeded to tie her hands to the heater, wrapping the duct tape over and over. The awkward position made everything hurt even worse. Her arms already ached from being raised in the air. Not to mention the tape felt like it was cutting off her circulation. She had nowhere to go now.

"Now you sit here and wait like a good little girl."

What? Where was he going...and why?

Maybe he saw the question in her expression because she didn't have the courage to ask it out loud. "I saw your little friends following us. I can't have them finding you. Not when I have so many delicious plans in store for you."

He gripped her neck, squeezing, leaning closer. "Do you remember the beautiful notes I wrote? Do you remember all the details of your punishment? Because I plan to do that and more. When I'm through with you, you will never disrespect me again."

He let go of her, propelling her backward so hard, her head hit the wall. The knock to her skull brought the focus of the pain to her head instead of her elbow and wrists. It affected her so much, her eyes blurred and a dull ringing in her ears erupted. Before she could avoid what he planned to do next, he shoved a piece of duct tape over her mouth. It dug into the sides of her mouth, causing intense agony as he started wrapping it around her head. He wrapped it around her head and face several times, making it as tight as he had her wrists.

Cruel, savage bastard!

She heard the door close more than she saw it. It took longer than she liked for her vision to clear.

Poor Abby and Bri. They had no warning he was coming for them next.

But Abby had a gun. Bri had a knife. They wouldn't go down without a fight. Of course, she didn't want to see either of them get hurt. Not because of her.

Ugh. And the Mace Bri had given her, she had forgotten to grab it before she left this morning. That would've come in handy.

Screaming would be useless. She yanked on her hands, knowing that was pointless as well. She had no way to escape or call for help.

She was a sitting duck, waiting for him to come back and torture her.

17

RIDER TUNED ABBY OUT when she informed them of her last sight of Junelle. Why would he want to hear more when none of it was good? The only thing he had paid attention to was which street they'd last seen her. Because that's where he'd pick up the trail.

It felt like an hour to reach their destination when it was less than ten minutes. The street was deserted. But by the one-sided conversation Tate was having—he'd taken it off speaker—he knew where they were.

Rider saw Abby and Bri appear from the opposite end. They met in the middle.

"I'm not sure if they dipped into one of these buildings," Abby stated, pointing to both walls surrounding them, "or if he ventured down to that end." She tossed a hand toward the way they had come from. "We looked both ways down there, but we didn't see much on the street."

"So we split up." Stromberg took a step closer to Bri, taking a hold of her hand. "Briella, sweetheart, why don't you and Abby head back down the street one more time? We'll handle the buildings."

Abby threw a hand to her hip. "We can help look in the buildings too. We checked the street. They aren't there. If they were, they're out of sight by now."

"What he's saying, Abby," Tate emphasized her name as if she were in deep trouble, "is we don't want you two around this area. You didn't pause that long for them to get all the way down this street. He had to have dipped into one of these buildings. Unless you think he did make it to the other side toward the street."

Abby shook her head, her arm falling to her side, though the irritation didn't lessen even though her body language suggested otherwise. "They would've had to go into a full run to make it to the other end of this street. I agree, I think they went into one of these buildings. Standing here arguing about who goes where is wasting time."

"I agree," Rider interjected before Tate could go further into hollering at Abby. "You two take that building," he said to the right, "I'll check this one. Don't take too long arguing about where those two are going." He jabbed a finger at Abby and Bri. "Because Junelle's life depends on it."

Then he walked away, letting them handle the rest on their own.

He tried the first door, finding it locked. The second door opened, not a creak, peep, or sound occurring.

"Did you hear anything before you looked down this street? A door opening or something?" Rider shouted toward the ladies.

"No. If I would have, we would've started with one of the buildings," Abby replied.

Rider stepped inside and pulled his gun out of its holster, raising it shoulder level as the door swung shut behind him. It made a short clang at the end. So either The

Ghost made sure it shut without a sound or he didn't come in this way.

He was about to find out.

Because he wasn't leaving this area until he searched every nook and cranny of both buildings. Abby was right. If he dragged Junelle to the end of the street, they were long gone by now. They had to be in one of the buildings or putting serious distance between them.

God, he hoped it was the former. The latter would make his job harder, and his mind to go faster into a tailspin.

He walked with careful, yet quiet footsteps down the hallway, trying doors as he went. Some were locked. Some were unlocked, but empty.

At the end, he debated left or right. He took a right, finding that side clear of anyone. Then ventured toward the left, finding the same thing. When he hit the end, he backtracked a few feet and turned down the next hallway, checking doors as he went along. Same thing as before. Locked or unlocked and empty.

It was an office building of some kind. Though abandoned or something as most rooms had desks and filing cabinets and such but not a lot of clutter as if people utilized them.

When he got to another intersecting hallway, he paused. Did he go straight, right, or left? Decisions, decisions. The longer he took, the more Junelle's life was at risk.

He'd start to the left as it was shorter than the right, then head right, followed by continuing straight. The two doors to the left were both locked. He made it a few steps away when he heard a noise.

His feet froze as he strained his ears. He wasn't quite sure what he'd heard. Turning his head, he stared at both doors he'd just tried. Both were locked.

But hell, that didn't mean anything. This man, The Ghost, was not an idiot. He'd already murdered in one city without anyone the wiser, moved, and started up in another city until it all started to unravel. Locking a door wouldn't require a mastermind to figure out how to unlock it, especially if one had a key.

He stopped at the first door, jiggling the knob. Then he listened, putting his ear closer to the door. He waited at least ten seconds before moving on to the other door, repeating the same process. This time, within two seconds of jiggling the knob, he heard it. A muffled sound. He wasn't quite sure what it was, but he wasn't going to ignore it.

"Junelle?! Is that you?!" he shouted, rattling the knob harder. He froze. That had been a dumb move to holler. Was that really her? If so, was she alone? Would he hurt her now that he knew Rider was closing in on them?

Shit!

No time to waste now. He backed up and rammed his shoulder into the door, grunting. It didn't budge. Not even an inch, and now his shoulder hurt like hell. New tactic. His foot. He backed up again, this time kicking at the door. That did nothing but jam his knee, pain rising from his foot and up through his body. It didn't matter. He repeated the hard kicks three more times before he managed to rip the door open, taking some of the frame with it.

He zeroed in on her right away, tied up against the wall. After shoving the broken door out of the way, he ran to her with the gun down by his side but still secure in his hand.

"I got you. I got you. I got you." He couldn't have stopped himself from repeating that if he tried. Because damn it, he did have her! He found her and he wouldn't let anything happen to her.

The duct tape tied around her mouth was too tight. At

least attempting to get it off with one hand, so he was forced to set his gun down. He had to be careful unwrapping the tape. She winced every now and again when the sticky part wouldn't let go of her hair.

"Shit. I almost have it. Hold on."

A few seconds later, he got it all off. The worst part had been the last piece covering her mouth. He knew it had hurt like a bitch when he ripped it off. She inhaled a few deep breaths before crying out with relief.

"Abby and Bri? Are they okay? He knew they were following me. He went to go...to go hurt them."

"They're fine. They're with Stromberg and Tate. Oh, baby," he said, cupping her cheeks, "I can't believe I found you. Thank God I found you."

She tried to wiggle her hands. "Get my hands, please. It hurts."

Taking the duct tape off her wrists was going to take a lot longer than her mouth had. He'd gotten a tiny portion unwrapped when Junelle shouted, "Behind you!"

He turned in time to dodge the sweep of the knife coming at him. Then he kicked at The Ghost, hitting him square in the knee, causing him to fall.

Triumph wasn't as near as he thought when he went toward the man to secure him. The Ghost popped up, not appearing in pain in the slightest from the jab to his knee. They stood in a crouched position, both ready to attack. The only difference was The Ghost had a knife and he had nothing. Not even his weapon because he had set it down on the floor. The Ghost had the upper hand and he knew it.

"I'm not going to let you ruin this for me."

Rider gave a short laugh. "You'll have to kill me before I let you touch one inch of her. And I sure in the hell ain't going to make it easy on you."

The Ghost swiped the knife in the air, missing him. But he felt the whoosh of air hit his face. It had been a close one.

"I'm more sufficient with a knife than you'll ever know."

Rider didn't doubt that. So far, every victim that they knew of, he'd used a knife. He felt very confident with one.

"Without your gun, you're going to lose. I promise you that." The Ghost jerked his hand toward the ground where his gun lay. "Go ahead and try for it. I'll gut you like a pig before your hand even touches it."

The man's arrogance would be his downfall. Rider knew it without a doubt. Because he refused to believe he'd lose this battle. He couldn't. Not with Junelle's life on the line. If he lost this, the man would torture her, and he couldn't allow that to happen. Not to his sweet, beautiful June Bug.

"I'm not afraid of your knife. I've been up close and personal with one before. It didn't take me down then, and I won't let one take me down now."

Hell, not wholly true. That knife had nearly taken his life. But, in the end, he'd survived. He won. If he didn't think positively, he'd lose.

The Ghost made a mad rush at him. The movement did surprise him, not expecting such a random movement. But not enough to disorient him. He blocked the knife with his forearm, feeling the sharp device slice him, but not do too much damage. His other hand jabbed hard into The Ghost's stomach, causing him to double over and grunt.

But neither bowed down to the other.

It came down to a battle of who was stronger, especially when The Ghost managed to knock them both to the floor with him on top. He raised the knife and swung down. Rider reached up to stop it, pushing hard against the resistance.

He exerted as much strength as The Ghost did. One pushing down, the other trying to push away. The muscles in his arms burned. His teeth ached from gritting them together. His entire life—the one he knew he was always meant to live with Junelle—flashed before his eyes. He didn't want to lose that. Not a moment of it.

He pushed back harder. The knife didn't move an inch. It crept closer and closer to his face. One wrong move, one tiny muscle failed him and it would penetrate right through his eye and deep into his brain.

It wasn't the shot that rang out that startled him. Or maybe it was. But it all happened in a split second. A gunshot echoed through the tiny room. The body above him became dead weight, making it too much for him to hold up any longer.

He half-groaned, half-screamed when the knife dug into his shoulder. Damn it. It felt like the same area as the last knife wound he'd suffered several months ago.

"Rider!" Junelle hollered. "Rider! Oh my god, are you all right? Rider?"

"I'm fine. It's okay."

And for the most part it was. He'd survived a knife to the shoulder before. What was one more time?

With the little strength he had left, he pushed and rolled the body off him.

Junelle screamed again, this time more high-pitched.

"He stabbed you! It's all my fault. I'm sorry. Don't—"

He scrambled to his feet, reaching her side in an instant. His hand brushed her cheek, quieting her down. "Shh, baby. I'm okay. Nothing is your fault. Hell, you saved my life. I'm apparently oh for two when it comes to saving someone."

She chuckled, shaking her head. "That's not funny, Rider. And you did save me. You're here. You found me."

Yeah, well, he wasn't the one who shot the gun and killed the bad guy. Just like with Bri, he wasn't the one to kill that bad guy either. Both women had saved themselves, and quite spectacularly.

Rider glanced back at The Ghost. Blood seeped from his head. If he wasn't mistaken, the wetness he felt on his face was blood that had sprayed when the bullet penetrated The Ghost's skull. Odd how that feeling only surfaced now and not when it initially happened.

"Where did you learn how to shoot like that?" Because damn, what a shot! He couldn't have been prouder. She had saved them both.

"Just now. I've never fired a weapon before."

He stared at her for a moment, processing that information. All he could come up with was luck had been on their side today.

Then he looked at her wrists. They were still bound by duct tape. Though, somehow she had managed to get herself free from the heater.

She'd fired the gun with her hands tied together, and managed a head shot. What an incredible woman.

"I'm sorry, baby. This is going to hurt."

Tears brimmed to the corner of her eyes, but she held up her hands and he started to unwrap the duct tape. It felt like it took ages. He tried his best to go slow when he neared the portion attached to her skin. He knew it still hurt like hell by the strain on her face. But he had done it. She was free.

She rubbed her wrists a few times before reaching up toward the knife, then hesitated to touch it.

"We need to get you to the hospital. You have a knife embedded in your shoulder."

"Yeah, it hurts like hell."

A noise behind him caught his attention. Then he heard a familiar, annoying voice.

"Don't take it out. Let the doctors handle it."

Rider twisted to see Tate and Stromberg enter the room. Good call by Tate. He wouldn't remove it. He'd yet to brave looking at the knife and he had no idea if it hit a vital area. The last thing he wanted to do was bleed out when he was a block away from the hospital.

Stromberg stepped around The Ghost and helped Rider stand up. He appreciated the help, but he wasn't going to stand there while Stromberg also helped Junelle to her feet. He needed to feel useful for a moment.

He blocked Stromberg's way, heard a short chuckle, then held out a hand, pulling Junelle to her feet.

She nearly hugged him, then stopped when she saw the knife. "Come on. I can't stand to see that."

Tate halted their exit. "As much as I'd love to see you walk down the street with a knife sticking out of your chest, I'm sure other people will freak out. Let's call an ambulance."

Another good call.

The world was starting to blur a bit. When he swayed, he wondered if the knife had hit something vital, and even though he hadn't taken it out, he was losing a lot of blood.

Junelle's arm went around his waist, holding him up. "Don't you dare die on me." She sniffed. "I lost my brother. I won't lose you too."

That's right. The bastard lying on the floor killed Jason. In that moment, he wanted to kill the man himself. Pull the trigger until every last bullet was embedded inside his chest.

"I'm sorry, Junelle."

She frowned. "For what?"

"For everything." Then he leaned harder on her, closing his eyes. It made it easier to block out her despair and desperation.

Some demon inside him felt responsible for Jason's

death. If he'd found the suspect sooner, none of this would've happened.

He could blame nobody but himself. No doubt, deep inside, she blamed him too.

As soon as they made it to the emergency room, they whisked Rider to a separate area in the hospital. No doubt the OR. She followed a nurse to a quiet room where the nurse looked at the few injuries she had. Marks around her wrists from the duct tape too tight. No blood was evident, but she'd have heavy bruising soon. A bandage went on her stomach where he'd shoved the knife in when they were leaving the hospital. Not deep enough where it required stitches. The same applied to the small cut on her neck.

All in all, she came out quite unscathed. Hopefully, Rider came out the same way. He'd been alert—for the most part—the entire ambulance ride. He'd been quiet, not saying much, but his eyes had opened and closed enough to know he hadn't passed out.

Stromberg and Tate had stayed with the body. She figured at some point she'd have to give a statement about everything that happened. She didn't look forward to it, though she knew it needed to be done. Sooner rather than later worked fine for her. But she knew it wouldn't happen right away. Not with the commotion of dealing with his body.

When she was finished with the nurse, she walked out to the emergency room waiting area and stood there. Not dazed, but frightened. She had to go see her parents and she didn't want to. The devastation that would be on their face. The grief. Something that hadn't hit her yet. She hadn't had any time to process the fact she'd been kidnapped and nearly killed.

"Hey, you okay?"

Junelle turned her attention to the soft voice coming from her right. Abby smiled, laying a comforting hand on her shoulder. "Tell us what you need."

Bri stood by her, displaying the same gentle smile. She still didn't know these two very well, but she knew they would always be a part of her life from here on out. Best friends, in fact. They saved her life, and she wouldn't accept anything less from them but besties for life.

Words failed her, despite that.

Her mouth wouldn't work.

Her mind lost all thought.

Tears rose to the surface, then rained down without being able to stop them.

"Tate said Rider suffered a minor injury and he'd be fine. Did something happen?" Abby said, leaning closer. The grip on her shoulder also increased.

"My brother..." She had to choke out the words.

At those two words, both women converged on her, cocooning her in a hug. She let the tears empty out of her. How long they stood there, she had no idea. Somehow she found herself being escorted to the ICU. It had to be done, but she dragged her feet the entire way.

Her parents were by the nurses' station when they entered the area.

"Oh, Junelle!" Her mother cried, slamming her arms around her.

She clung to her mother in the same way she gripped her back.

"My sweet baby girl. I was so worried about you." Her

mother pulled away to see her face. "What happened? You were with Jason and then you weren't."

By the grimace on her mother's lips, her face didn't look pretty. No doubt red marks and bruises from when he tied the tape around her mouth. It still hurt, even to speak.

Her bottom lip trembled, unable to find the right words. How did she tell her mother it was her fault Jason had died? She'd done nothing to stop the madman from hurting him. She'd been useless and weak.

Bri stepped closer. "The man who was stalking her showed up. Made her leave with him." Her mother's eyes rounded. In shock? In fear? The flash of emotions was hard to decipher. Maybe Bri couldn't figure it out either as she rushed on. "He's dead. He can't hurt anyone else."

"Mom, it's my fault Jason died. He put something in Jason's IV. Something that he said would cause his heart to stop. I did nothing to stop him."

Her mother shook her as she cried, "You did *nothing* wrong! Do you hear me? I could've lost you today. We nearly lost Jason."

She blinked, replaying her mother's last sentence. "Nearly? What do you mean?"

A sweet smile lit up her mother's face. "His heart did stop. He died. It was the worst minute of my life watching them try to revive him, but they did. He's alive, Junelle. Your brother is a fighter. Now that we know something was injected, we'll tell the doctors. Make sure nothing happens again."

With that, her mother rushed to the nurses to relay the information. Her dad took that moment to step forward and get his own hug.

"I'm so glad you're okay, pumpkin."

She snuggled into her father's embrace, feeling the same

exact sentiment. What a horrible week, but it was all over now. The bad guy was dead and no one else could hurt her or anyone in her family.

The rest of the day flew by in a blur. Rider wasn't in surgery long, and once he woke up, he wanted to be released. The doctor said no. He didn't listen until she insisted he rest. Then promised to stay by his side.

Or maybe it was the drugs they gave him to lessen the pain, but he calmed down and closed his eyes.

She was true to her word. She stayed by his side the entire night. The room had a nice reclining chair in the corner for her to sleep in. Though she would've crashed in any kind of chair that they had.

The next morning, she left him after he woke up to check on her brother. Still the same condition as before. It was better than it getting worse or him dying altogether. She'd take no change over anything else.

From there, she went back to Rider's room to see him dressed and ready to leave.

"Did the doctor say you could leave?"

He grinned at her, and by the mischievous look, the doctor hadn't. "I'm okay."

Maybe he thought he was, but if the doctor didn't approve it yet, he should stay.

The sparkle of happiness that he had disappeared. "Is everything okay with Jason?"

"Of course. He's doing well. And I want you to be well too. If the doctor says—"

He brushed her cheek with his left hand. "I'm okay. But I'm not a fan of hospitals, not after being in one for so long. I can rest at home as well as I can here."

"But are you going to rest?"

He shifted his right shoulder a bit, wincing at the slight

movement. "Yes, because it hurts like a son of a bitch. I'm sidelined at work again, so the faster I heal, the faster I can get back to normal duties. I hate sitting at a desk all day long."

"I'll take you home then."

He shook his head. "You don't have to."

Of course she didn't have to. She wanted to. Unless he was saying he didn't want her to.

"You haven't been home yourself. I made you sleep all night in an uncomfortable chair. You probably want to go home, shower, relax in your own space."

More like he wanted to give her an easy out. He didn't want her anymore. Not in his home. Not in his life. Because otherwise she didn't know why he was acting like this.

"You're right." And she wasn't going to rip the rest of her heart out on her own by asking questions. He'd done that just fine.

He frowned. "Thank you for staying by my side."

"It was no problem. I'm glad your injuries were minor. I'll talk to you later."

"Yeah, of course."

Then she left before she broke down in tears in front of him. She had no idea what had gone wrong. Why he seemed to be pushing her away?

A lot had happened in a short span. Maybe she needed to give him time and space and then they could talk. About them. About their future.

Because she wanted a future with him. She'd messed up five years ago. She refused to make the same mistakes again.

Communication was key.

She'd make him talk about his feelings sooner or later.

18

I'll talk to you later. The last sentence Junelle had said to him. Two weeks ago.

Two. Weeks. Ago.

Their last conversation replayed in his mind over and over, wondering where he'd gone wrong. He hadn't meant to shove her out of his life or make her feel that way. It had been a stressful night, and he'd felt guilty making her stay with him. Her brother ranked higher than him. Not to mention the guilt and turbulent emotions she had killing someone. He'd wanted to give her time to process all of that. To have a moment to herself instead of monopolizing all her time. Not once did he think it would remove her from his life.

He had no idea how time passed in a blink of an eye and he hadn't said one word to her. Not at the hospital when he visited Jason. She had never been there at the same time as him. As if she knew when to avoid going so she wouldn't have to see him. Not at the precinct when he went in a few times to check on the progress of some of his cases. He knew she had to give a statement, and that she'd been there a few times herself. Missed her each time. And he'd always been ushered back out by his captain.

Well, no more. He'd taken two weeks off to recover and he was as recovered as he was going to get. Yeah, he still needed to watch the stitches. Yeah, he was still on restrictions for another month or so. But, no, he wasn't going to sit on his ass at home when he could sit on his ass at work just the same. He understood he couldn't go out in the field yet. Fine. But he could use his hands and voice and work from his desk. Half the time, that's how his job operated anyway.

Tate, Stromberg, Cramer, and Jackson had wrapped The Ghost case with a big red bow. Well, as much as they could. After they ran the man's fingerprints in the system, a slew of unsolved cases popped up all over the country. Murders that occurred years ago. None in the past two though. Which told Rider he'd gotten better at avoiding leaving evidence. They still had no name to put to his face, but it didn't matter in the long run. The man couldn't hurt anyone else. They'd passed all the information they had to the FBI and said farewell to the massive investigation they had on their hands now. The good thing about linking him to the unsolved murders was those families would have some answers. Finally. Some peace of mind the killer had been caught.

That's why he did what he did. Give people closure. Give them safety. Give them knowledge and power to fight back. Because not all cases were closed with a dead suspect. Most of the time it went to court. That was never an easy battle. He was glad this one would be.

He had just sat down at his desk when his phone rang. Janice. Not Junelle. He'd take what he could get at this point.

"Hi, Janice."

"He's awake."

That's all he needed to hear to get to the hospital. A flurry of activity bounced around Jason all day long. Visitors coming and going. Most were family, but a few friends—like him.

Despite seeing Junelle amongst everyone, he still managed not to get a word out of her. At least, not aimed at him.

Whatever odd thing going on between them was still there. It bothered the hell out of him, but he didn't know how to fix it.

Although today had meant to be his first day back to work, he never returned after he got the phone call. He had wanted to give Jason space, not wanting to overwhelm him, but he found himself returning that evening after hours. A quick flash of his badge had the night nurse on duty letting him in.

He didn't knock in case Jason was asleep and even opened the door as quietly as he could. But it was for naught. Jason was sitting up in bed staring at the TV, though the volume was on low.

"Hey, man." Jason sounded tired, along with his eyes looking like the dead. He wouldn't stay long. Despite being in a coma for as long as he had, his friend needed rest. Tons of it.

"Hey." He sat down in a chair by the bed closest to the window. "How you feeling?"

"Like I was stabbed a billion times." Jason chuckled, then winced, groaning. "Laughing hurts. Everything hurts, man. The wounds are healing and looking good the doc says, but shit, it still hurts."

"Dude, you were stabbed five times." Not to state the obvious, but...

Jason grinned. Rider could tell it took a lot of energy for him not to laugh as well. "I got you beat."

He cocked a brow. "Are we seriously going to have a showdown over who got stabbed more?"

"I'm just saying..." Another chuckle escaped along with a wince. "You love to claim you won tug-of-war in our senior year."

He sat up straight, pointing a finger at him. "I did. Me and my team won!"

"Your foot stepped over the line first."

"But your team all crumbled to the ground first."

"But your foot crossing the line makes you the loser."

"The hell it does! I remained standing along with my entire team."

More laughter filled the air by both of them, except low moans of pain filtered out from Jason. "Don't make me laugh, asshole."

Rider relaxed in his chair. "You started it."

Jason glanced at the TV. "Thanks for protecting my sister. I can't believe what happened. What I let—"

"Hey," he leaned forward again, "you didn't *let* anything happen. It's not your fault. If anyone protected anyone it was Junelle saving my ass. Like I told her, I'm oh for two protecting people. I suck at it."

Jason's lips widened in a grin, but he refrained from laughing. "Still. Thank you."

He didn't want Jason's thanks. Junelle had been the one to pull the trigger.

"Did she tell you everything that happened?"

Hopefully she had because then he wouldn't. He already had nightmares about it. Talking about it wouldn't help. Of course, Jason had a right to know.

"She did. I'm glad that bastard is dead. She is too. I can tell even if she didn't say it out loud."

Rider hoped that meant she wasn't struggling too much with what she had done.

"Did something happen between you two?"

Rider's brows drew together, weighing his words before speaking. What did he mean by the question? What had Junelle told him?

"I ask because you two didn't exchange one word earlier today. Why not?"

That was an excellent question. One he didn't have an answer for.

"No clue. I don't know where it all went wrong."

Jason stared at him, his brows pleating, deep in thought. "Meaning it wasn't wrong the entire time I was out of it?"

Rider chuckled. "Not sure you want to hear how I... *comforted* your sister."

A wicked grin erupted on Jason's face. "I don't, man, but it is nice to hear you were comforting her. You two were meant for each other. Don't mess it up."

It might've already happened somehow. Unwittingly.

He didn't know how to respond to that either, so he said nothing. Silence filled the room. A long few minutes passed, though it wasn't an uncomfortable silence.

"You know what I've noticed since you got here?" Jason asked. "You haven't rubbed your chest once. It's nice to see that habit has stopped. But I get it now. I get why you did it."

Hell, he didn't even remember when he stopped doing it. He couldn't even remember the last time he'd felt the phantom pain. It was better than nice that that habit had ceased. More like wonderful. It hadn't been something he liked people witnessing. A sign of weakness more than anything else.

"Well don't copy me. Even though I know you love to. As I'm the better man."

A snort erupted from Jason followed by a low groan. "I'm going to get you back for every time you've made me laugh tonight."

And he was a-okay with that. Because he *was* laughing. Way better than being dead.

"But I need you to leave now."

He flinched by the abrupt dismissal.

Another grin punctured Jason's face. "Not because I'm not enjoying your company, but I think you have somewhere else you need to be. Someone else you need to be talking to."

Junelle.

He wasn't wrong.

Except Rider had no idea what to say. Since he didn't know what he'd done wrong.

"It's late."

He'd let Jason interpret that any way he wanted to. It was late and he should leave him to rest. It was late and he couldn't possibly visit Junelle tonight.

His chair scraped against the floor as he stood up. He smiled in goodbye and headed for the door.

Jason's words stopped him in his tracks, but he didn't turn around. "It's never too late."

LIFE WAS ALMOST BACK to normal. Junelle wanted to throw a party to celebrate. A small one. Nothing too extravagant or over-the-top. And when her brother was released from the hospital, she'd do that. Him surviving a deadly attack was cause for celebration.

Tonight, she decided to have her own mini celebration —party of one. She'd cracked open a bottle of wine earlier and was already on her second glass.

Maybe it was the wine going to her head. Or maybe it was the silence drowning her. Or even perhaps the ache that had centered deep in her heart and refused to go away. Whatever the reason, her mind wouldn't veer from Rider. What she should do. How she could start a conversation she was terrified to have.

Today would've been a good day to do it. He'd looked at her several times when they'd been in Jason's room. Yet, it had been full of people. And a hospital wasn't the best setting for such a serious chat. Of course, she could've made arrangements with him for later in the day. Instead, she went the chickenshit route. While some could interpret her drinking as wallowing in self-pity, she was going with a solo party.

And she could celebrate life in her bed just as well as the couch. It would be more comfortable. She clicked the remote to turn off the TV, then she grabbed the wine bottle from the coffee table and refilled her glass to the top. Hell, she'd bring the bottle with her. She didn't get more than a few steps away before her doorbell rang.

The sudden noise startled her, causing some of the wine to splash over the side of the rim. Thank goodness she'd chosen white wine tonight and not red.

Setting both bottle and glass down on the coffee table, she hesitated to move closer to the door.

Who would be visiting so late at night? The last time she'd checked her phone—something she'd fiddled with all night long—it had told her it was nearing ten o'clock. That was twenty minutes ago.

Well, whoever it was, she would not cower in fear. She'd

survived a stalker and serial killer, she could handle whoever was on the other side of the door. When she glanced through the peephole to see Rider standing there, she changed her mind. She couldn't handle this visitor.

She still had no idea what to say, or what had gone wrong between them.

After such a beautiful, erotic evening together only to go radio silent for two weeks, it made no sense.

But she couldn't ignore him either.

She opened the door, hoping he couldn't see the panic.

They stared at each other.

Until he cracked a smile. "Can I come in?"

"Yes, of course." For goodness' sake. She needed to get her senses back.

She gestured him inside, then closed and locked the door behind him. His gaze darted around the room, lingering on the wine glass and bottle, before turning toward her.

"I can come back tomorrow if you're busy."

Drinking by herself wasn't classified as being busy. But maybe this was him telling her he was as nervous as she was.

"It's fine. Is everything okay?" Her parents would've called if something had happened to Jason. If he somehow had taken a turn for the worse.

"No." He shook his head while his eyes flashed regret. "I didn't mean to make you worry something was wrong. I..." He inhaled a large breath and then let it out. "Somehow things got awkward between us and I'm here wondering why."

At least one of them had the courage to speak up. She shrugged, having absolutely no clue.

But her nonchalance about it didn't work in her favor. At all. The indentation between his eyebrows increased.

"I'm sorry, Junelle."

He'd said that once already. He'd lumped that apology all into one. And he'd had nothing to be sorry about. It had confused her then, and it continued to baffle her now.

"I don't understand. You have nothing to apologize for."

His eyes widened as he lifted his arms and threw them down in frustration. "Nothing? Are you kidding me? You killed a man because I couldn't protect you. He nearly killed Jason when I should've found him way before then. I put you in danger—"

She rushed forward, laying a hand over his chest. In the same spot he used to rub, which he hadn't done once yet tonight. Normally, it would've been the first thing he'd do when the talk turned in this direction. She couldn't remember when he stopped doing it, but she found herself touching the same spot nonetheless.

"I believe we're both blaming ourselves for things we had no control over. So I think we should both stop doing that."

A tiny grin emerged on his face.

"I did kill someone. Sometimes, when I'm sleeping, I relive it. Weirdly enough, I wouldn't classify it as a nightmare. More like a memory erupting in my dreams. I should feel guilty about killing him, but I don't. I feel guilty about a lot of things, but that's not one of them. He hurt my brother. He hurt you. And he wanted to hurt me. In ways that I know I would've struggled to deal with. But he couldn't do any of it because you got there first. You saved me. I saved you. I think we can call it even."

"I'm glad to hear that. I wish I could say I wasn't having nightmares, but I am. I see you tied to that heater. Scared, crying. I see the blood on your neck, and it goes from a trickle to a stream. I always wake up before you...you die, but I know that's where my mind wants to go."

His hand covered hers. The warmth from his touch filled up part of her soul that had chilled from his absence. "I don't know why we stopped talking these last two weeks. I've hated every second of it. What did I do wrong?"

"I thought I did something wrong. That morning you told me to leave. That I couldn't take you home. I thought..." She shrugged, struggling to find the right words.

He closed his eyes, shaking his head. Then they reopened as his other hand went around her waist and pulled her closer. "I'm an idiot, June Bug. A big, colossal idiot. I thought you wanted space. Needed space after everything that happened. I never meant to push you away. That wasn't my intention at all."

A small smile began to form. "Really? Did we have another communication mishap that could've been avoided?"

"It sounds like it." He pressed his lips to hers, and she welcomed the tender touch. "June Bug, that night was the best night of my life. I'm not saying five years ago wasn't good between us. Because it was. But that was puppy love compared to now. I bared my soul to you. I let go of everything and opened myself up. I swear I felt the same from you. That night was more than just a night to me. It was everything. It told me I would fight for you. It told me that I could not lose you again—for any reason. I love you, June Bug. With my entire heart, body, and soul. I'm not walking away this time or letting you either."

His wondrous words were everything she always wanted to hear and more.

"I love you too, Rider. More than you could ever know. I

wasn't going to walk away this time. I was trying to find the courage to tell you how I felt, worried you didn't feel the same."

"Well, I do."

"I knew you were the one from the first moment I fell in love with you. It was fate."

"Was it now?" He grabbed her around the waist and lifted her up. She wrapped her legs around him, holding on like the lifeline he was.

"Of course. Has it ever occurred to you what your first name is?"

His brow rose, his eyes twinkling with laughter. "It is my first name. I do know it."

She giggled, bending her head until her lips hit his neck. "Yeah, but the first letter..."

"Holy hell."

She lifted her head to see the amazement on his face. She knew it wasn't from the tiny kiss she had bestowed upon him. "Yeah, it was fate. *Jack* Rider. You were meant to be with me from the beginning."

"I won't argue with that logic. Does this mean we're naming our kids with their first name starting with J too?"

"Duh."

"Poor Jason. What happens if he finds a woman he loves whose name doesn't start with a J?"

"He'll be immediately disowned."

Rider's boisterous laugh filled her heart with joy. She wanted to hear so many more laughs coming from him until the day she died.

"I'm spending the night."

Abrupt conversation change, but she'd go along with it. She didn't even bother giving him crap for not asking her. The demand turned her on.

"Not just tonight. Every single night."

Her eyebrows lifted as her lips pursed together in a tight line. *This* she might want to comment on. "That sounds a lot like you're telling me you're moving in."

"I am." He moved forward toward the door, then swiveled around so she faced the alarm panel on the wall instead of him. "Set the alarm, June Bug."

Another demand, but one she wouldn't argue with. She wasn't sure why she wanted to argue about him moving in. The thought didn't bother her. To have Rider with her always, well, it's something she'd always dreamed about. To have it happen was wonderful news.

He carried her upstairs to her room, then laid her on the bed. His hands were quick as they divested her of all her clothes. His disappeared just as quickly. Then he was hovering above her, his eyes glittering with all the love he'd expressed moments before.

While she was wet and ready, his fingers played and teased her first. She wanted him deep inside, but words failed her. His fingers did their job well while his lips found her neck, peppering light kisses.

She should get back to the moving in conversation, but her mind had turned to mush. Then nothing but euphoria hit her senses as an orgasm tore through her. All that came out was the sound of his name.

"Yes, baby, I want to hear that again." He slammed inside of her, thrusting in and out with complete abandon. "I know you can get louder."

She giggled, meeting him thrust for thrust. "The neighbors might hear."

"I don't give a shit. Let them hear."

He stopped, his breathing heavy, and sat up, lifting her legs. "Tell me I'm moving in."

She moaned in reply. The sensations were building again. This one felt like it would be even bigger than the last time.

"Say it."

"Why not your apartment?"

He didn't move a muscle. "I don't care where we live, but we're staying together. From this night forward. Say it."

She lifted her hips when he didn't resume moving.

"I need to hear you say it. I need to know we're on the same page. There will be no further miscommunication between us ever again. I will not lose one second with you."

He wasn't demanding anything of her. He needed confirmation that they were picturing the same future together.

"Okay, fine. I'll say we're moving in together if you say we're getting married as soon as possible."

A devilish grin built as he dropped her legs and leaned closer until he could reach her lips. Then he was kissing her as if it'd be the last one they'd ever share. Slow, beautiful thrusts resumed.

"My sweet, delectable June Bug, I would marry you tomorrow if I knew your mother wouldn't have a heart attack at the thought."

Her laughter was smothered by another deep kiss. He wasn't wrong in that assessment. But they were on the same page.

His kiss didn't stop, his tongue dueling and playing with hers. One hand gripped the pillow next to her as the other attached to her hair. His thrusts were deep and hard. One after another. The bliss swirled inside of her until she knew she was close. He sensed it, so attuned to her movements and her low moans she couldn't keep in.

"Say my name, baby. Scream it. I need to hear it."

Her hands latched onto his ass, her nails digging in as

his name tore from her lips. He pumped two more times, stiffening and whispering her name as he hit the pinnacle himself.

His entire body relaxed into hers, his lips trailing tenderly up and down her neck.

"I don't think it's fair I scream your name and you whisper mine."

He lifted his head, another sly grin puncturing his lips. "We can't have that. Totally not fair. I guess I have to love you again until I manage to do that."

She would not argue with that.

"I love you, June Bug."

"Not as much as I love you."

She'd have to show him for the rest of his life—despite her mistake five years ago—that her words were true.

EPILOGUE

Four months later

JASON SAT BACK, twisting back and forth to get the kink out of his back. It didn't work, of course. That damn pain had been there since he'd been released from the hospital. It wasn't as if he'd been stabbed in the back, or that the knife penetrated all the way through to the other side. But the pain emerged and refused to go away.

Maybe it had been from the lack of movement for so long. Three weeks in a coma, then another week before they released him. Even when he got home, it had been a hard recovery. He'd been on so many damn restrictions it had been easier to stay in bed than do anything else.

But he was off all restrictions. While he loved working out and keeping in shape, he wasn't back to full strength. It was a good thing he owned his construction company. He could delegate and make everyone do everything instead of doing it himself. Though he loved building and working with his hands, it killed him not to jump into their latest project. He'd be back at it in no time, doing everything he'd done before the attack. He wouldn't have it any other way.

Life was good.

Better than those horrible few weeks so many months ago.

"You look like you're moping over here? Why are you moping?" Rider scooted a chair out and sat down, setting a fresh beer bottle in front of him. "It's my wedding day. You're not allowed to mope. Next month when Bri and Stromberg get married, you can mope there."

He picked it up, gesturing toward him in thanks. "I'm not moping. I'm taking a break."

"I haven't seen you break dancing or anything yet."

Yeah, well, he wasn't much of a dancer to begin with, and Rider knew that. It didn't matter if it was Rider and Junelle's wedding day, he needed quite a few more beers before he got down and dirty on the dance floor.

Plus, he still had aches and pains that hadn't gone away.

His free hand reached up and rubbed his left side. Rider's gaze zeroed in on the movement. Shit.

"I'm sorry, man. I didn't realize you were hurting. We wouldn't be mad if you left early."

He dropped his hand. "It's not bad."

"So not actual pain?"

He cocked a brow, not trying to hide his irritation at the dumb question. Of course it was real pain. Why would he fake it?

"Like when I used to rub my chest. It wasn't actual pain. It was like a phantom pain. Like a gesture I couldn't stop even when I told myself to stop doing it."

"I wish it was a phantom pain."

By the morose expression Rider answered with, he was letting him know he really didn't wish that.

"It's not that bad. My back is bugging me. I need a few minutes and then I'll continue to mingle."

Rider winced, then stood up. "I'm holding you to that. I see Ms. Vanhouser is walking straight toward my dad. I better intercept her."

"It wouldn't be such a bad thing if your dad started dating again, Rider."

The disgusted look he gave him was enough to tell him Rider disagreed.

Jason sat a few more minutes, polished off the beer, and stood up to find another one. It was time to get this party started. But first, he needed to get a bit more drunk and then he'd make a fool of himself on the dance floor.

He ordered another beer from the open bar and waited two seconds before it appeared before him. When he turned around, he bumped into a woman with her eyes glued to her phone.

His chin had hit her head, and it throbbed. By the way she rubbed the top of her head, hers wasn't fairing much better.

"I'm so sorry. I didn't see you."

She smiled. The force of it hit him in the gut. "I suppose I should apologize as well. I wasn't paying attention. Crime never sleeps, so work never stops."

He took that to mean she worked with Rider at the precinct. He was still trying to get to know all the new people in Rider's life. Hell, he was invited to a wedding next month to people he barely knew. But all he needed to know was they had been there for Junelle when she needed it the most. They were getting the best wedding present on the planet.

"I'm Jason." He held out his hand. "Brother to the bride."

She eyed his hand for a moment, then accepted it. She

released it just as quickly. Odd, but whatever. Not everyone liked to shake hands.

"Victoria." Then she blinked while shaking her head once. "Friends to the groom." Her phone pinged, producing a grimace he knew all too well.

Rider had displayed the same kind of face when he needed to leave for a crime scene.

"I hope you don't have to leave." Because it was never fun having to leave a party early.

She frowned.

Unless she wasn't having fun.

He gestured toward her phone still clutched in her hand. The incessant pinging said she would have to. "You sound popular right now."

"Popular is but an adjective. It doesn't mean much in the grand scheme of things." Then she lifted her phone and forced out a grin. At least it looked forced to him. "But yes, it appears I may have to leave."

What an odd woman. Jason found it hard to believe Rider was friends with her. Of course, they hadn't talked for quite a few years, and in the last few months he'd found Rider had changed in a few ways. Hell, he'd changed himself. Life did that to a person. Though, they still managed to jump back into their friendship as if they had never been apart.

The fast, upbeat song that had been playing stopped. The slow, melodic tunes of a love song started.

"Would you like to dance before you leave?"

She looked at him as if he'd asked her to remove all her clothes. Offended and pissed off. First, he hadn't had enough to drink to even want to go on the dance floor. Second, the woman intrigued him so he had thought—what the hell. Ask her to dance. So much for spontaneity.

"No, thank you."

Then she turned around and left him standing there befuddled. It wasn't often women turned him down. Well, the conceited part of him would say it never happened. There was always a first time for everything.

Rider reappeared by his side, and he knew why the laughter circled the air.

"Shut up."

"Did you really ask her to dance? Mr. I-never-dance."

"It was for the best." He took a large gulp of the ice-cold beer. "It would've never worked out between us. What would happen if that dance would've been the best dance of my life? I would've had to turn down any other contact with her."

Rider gestured to the barkeep for a beer and leaned on the bar. "Do tell why you would've had to do that."

"Her name is Victoria. I'd be disowned from my family if I don't marry someone with a name that starts with J. You know this. Junelle would've never married you if your name wasn't Jack."

Rider laughed. "Nobody even calls me Jack."

"Doesn't matter. It's still your first name."

"Are you telling me I would've never had a chance with your sister if my name wasn't Jack?"

"It's the rule of the family. You got lucky."

Rider grinned. "No, it was fate."

"I didn't know you were such a romantic." They clinked their bottles together. "And it was fate that Victoria declined my dance. It would've never worked out with us in the long run."

The devious grin Rider gave him made no sense. "Fate will get you sooner or later."

Yeah, he hoped for later. He wasn't in the right mindset for dating anyhow.

The nightmares he had said so.

Hell, he even struggled during the day, not that he'd let anyone know that. How often he looked over his shoulder. How he didn't like people to get too close to him. He took wide births around people in a crowd. He never wanted to be snuck up on again.

That madman had nearly taken his life, and he'd also succeeded in taking his confidence. He might put on a good show for the world, but deep down, he had a hard time even leaving his house.

"Come on. Chug that beer and grab another. I want to dance, and I know your ass won't do it until you're good and drunk."

Sounded like a plan to him. Getting good and drunk. It would hold the nightmares at bay and squash his fears for just a moment.

Find out what happens in the next book, Vicious Consequences!

For Tate & Abby's story
Dark Consequences
A Consequences Novel, #1

Every choice has a consequence...

Detective Tate Powell lives for one thing: revenge against the man who killed his sister. But when he discovers that man is none other than his girlfriend Abby's brother, his world shatters.

Torn between loyalty to her troubled brother and her feelings for Tate, Abby faces an impossible choice. She must betray the man she loves to protect her family. Even if it means turning against Tate forever.

As Tate's thirst for vengeance spirals out of control, he risks losing Abby and damning his own soul. Will he choose retribution or redemption before he loses Abby forever?

With gut-wrenching twists and taut suspense, this gripping thriller will leave romantic suspense fans on the edge of their seats. Find out in the explosive first book of the Consequences series!

FOR WYATT & BRIELLA'S STORY
CRUEL CONSEQUENCES
A CONSEQUENCES NOVEL, #2

Some consequences can be so...cruel.

Working cold cases never bothered Detective Wyatt Stromberg—until one unimaginably brutal murder that haunts his dreams. Finding closure for the victim's sister Briella becomes an obsession. She's equally tormented by guilt that she failed her sister and is determined to ensure the killer faces justice.

As they grow dangerously close to the truth, and each other, the killer resurfaces, and he has his sights on Briella. Why now? Why allow a year to pass first? It doesn't matter—Wyatt vows to protect Briella no matter what. But the killer's sinister game of cat-and-mouse lurks around every corner, testing Wyatt's limits.

To save Briella, Wyatt must walk a tightrope between breaking protocol and breaking the law. With lives on the line, can he toe that precarious line before the killer checkmates them all?

With harrowing twists and turns, this gripping thriller will leave romantic suspense fans on the edge of their seats. Don't miss the next intense book in the Consequences series!

FOR JASON & VICTORIA'S STORY
VICIOUS CONSEQUENCES
A CONSEQUENCES NOVEL, #4

No good deed goes unpunished.

Jason Swanson thought he was done being a victim. After barely surviving an attack that left him jumping at shadows, he refuses to stand by when he witnesses a vicious assault. Except his heroism backfires when he's arrested for the crime. Worse, the lead detective is the same woman who shot him down at his best friend's wedding.

Detective Victoria Johansen is tough as nails when it comes to her job, even if she's awkward around everyone else. When she realizes she arrested the wrong man, she's strong enough to admit her mistake. What she doesn't expect is her growing attraction to Jason—a man who sees past her oddness to the woman beneath.

As their relationship deepens, the real killer emerges from the shadows, turning their investigation into a deadly game of cat and mouse. But they have no idea how close the danger really is. Or that the killer has been watching them all along.

Perfect for readers who crave pulse-pounding romantic suspense with jaw-dropping twists. One-click **Vicious Consequences** *now to start this edge-of-your-seat thriller today!*

ABOUT THE AUTHOR

I'm a *USA Today* Bestselling Author that loves to write contemporary romance and romantic suspense novels, although I am partial to romantic suspense. I even dabble in paranormal. Honestly, I love anything that has to do with romance. As long as there's a happy ending, I'm a happy camper. And insta-love...yes, please! I love baseball (Go Twins!) and creating awesome crafts. I graduated with a Bachelor's Degree in Criminal Justice, working in that field for several years before I became a stay-at-home mom. I have a few more amazing stories in the works. If you would like to learn more about me and my books, head to my website by scanning the QR code. Thanks for reading!

Scan me